the
clueless
girl's
guide
to being a
genius

the clueless girl's guide to being a genius

Janice Repka

Dutton Children's Books

An imprint of Penguin Group (USA) Inc.

DUTTON CHILDREN'S BOOKS
A division of Penguin Young Readers Group

Published by the Penguin Group | Penguin Group (USA) Inc., 375 Hudson Street,
New York, New York 10014, U.S.A. | Penguin Group (Canada), 90 Eglinton Avenue
East, Suite 700, Toronto, Ontario M4P 2Y3, Canada (a division of Pearson Penguin
Canada Inc.) | Penguin Books Ltd, 80 Strand, London WC2R 0RL, England | Penguin
Ireland, 25 St Stephen's Green, Dublin 2, Ireland (a division of Penguin Books Ltd) |
Penguin Group (Australia), 250 Camberwell Road, Camberwell, Victoria 3124, Australia
(a division of Pearson Australia Group Pty Ltd) | Penguin Books India Pvt Ltd, 11
Community Centre, Panchsheel Park, New Delhi - 110 017, India | Penguin Group (NZ),
67 Apollo Drive, Rosedale, Auckland 0632, New Zealand (a division of Pearson New
Zealand Ltd.) | Penguin Books (South Africa) (Pty) Ltd, 24 Sturdee Avenue, Rosebank,
Johannesburg 2196, South Africa | Penguin Books Ltd, Registered Offices: 80 Strand,
London WC2R 0RL, England

CIP Data is available.

Published in the United States by Dutton Children's Books, a division
of Penguin Young Readers Group, 345 Hudson Street, New York, New York 10014
www.penguin.com/youngreaders

Designed by IRENE VANDERVOORT

ISBN: 987-0-525-42333-1
Printed in USA | First Edition | 10 9 8 7 6 5 4 3 2 1

for Daisy

the
clueless
girl's
guide
to being a
genius

1 Aphrodite Wigglesmith
Gets It Started

Here's something fun you can do. First, get out of your chair. (I'm trusting you on that.) Next, stand in an open space. (Trusting you again.) Now spin like a quantum mechanical particle. (Or a top or tornado, whatever.) Faster. Faster. STOP. Did you feel it? That slip-in-time moment when your brain hadn't caught up with your body and it felt like you were still spinning? I love that. It's like my body has outsmarted my brain, which is not easy to do. Excuse the pun, but my brain kind of has a mind of its own. If you put a math problem, no matter how hard, in front of my eyes it sets off this switch and I have to try to solve it. So my life's been a little weird, I guess you could say.

The weirdness started the day someone flushed a firecracker down a toilet in the boys' bathroom on the second floor of Carnegie Middle School. The potty shattered, a weak pipe burst, and sewage water rained into the school office below.

"Holy crap!" Principal DeGuy yelled to his secretary. "Get someone here fast."

My mother, Cecelia Wigglesmith, was the "plumber on call" that day. She loaded crescent wrenches and extra piping into her truck while I climbed into my car seat. Although only four years old, I was already a mini-version of my mother physically—petite, with pale skin and black hair. But intellectually, I was bored silly and hungering for stimulation. To keep busy on the way to the plumbing job, I counted each church we passed on the left and each bar we passed on the right and kept a working ratio.

A few miles later, a sign announced we had reached Carnegie Middle School, "home to the division champion wrestling team, the Carnegie Spiders." The school was ten times as long as my house and five times as wide. Inside the office, Mother set me down on a desk.

"You stay here while I find the shutoff valve," she said. She turned to the secretary. "I hope you don't mind keeping an eye on my daughter. I'll be back as soon as things are under control."

The secretary was also perched on top of a desk. She was wearing a flamingo pink dress and held up her right foot. Her right shoe, which must have dropped when she hopped up, was floating out the door. The smell alone would have reduced most four-year-olds to tears, but to me, it just smelled like Mother had come home from work.

After Mother left, a piece of soaked ceiling tile fell and splattered us with sewage water. The secretary screamed and I jumped. The office phones began to ring. I counted the number of rings. I counted the number of ceiling chunks that fell and the number of times we screamed and jumped. I found that: 5 rings + 1 splash = 1 scream + 1 jump.

"You've got a shattered toilet and a burst pipe in the boys' bathroom," Mother said when she returned.

"Can you fix it?" asked Principal DeGuy, following her. He was middle-aged, but most of his hair hadn't made it that far. What was left covered his lower head in a U-shape. "We're scheduled for state testing in the morning, so I can't cancel school tomorrow."

"Once the pipe's repaired, I'll have to bail," said Mother. "Pumps will only pull so many gallons per hour. You've got four inches of water on the first floor, eighteen in the basement. Goodness knows how long that could take."

"Three hours and twenty-five minutes," I said.

Despite his ample ears, Principal DeGuy did not seem to hear. "I'm not interested in what goodness knows," he told Mother. "How long will *you* need to get this water out?"

"Three hours and twenty-five minutes," I repeated.

"Whose child is this?"

Mother picked me up and held me against her hip. "She's mine. Do you have a calculator?" Principal De-Guy pulled out his computerized planner. Mother told him the formula to figure out how long it would take.

"Three hours and twenty-five minutes," he said.

They stared at me.

"How did you do that?" Mother asked.

I shrugged and counted the number of teeth in the principal's open mouth.

"You gave her the answer," he said.

"I'm sure it was just a coincidence," Mother replied. "Aphrodite is usually so quiet you don't know she's in the room."

A chunk of ceiling tile fell and splashed Principal DeGuy with water. The secretary screamed again.

"I'd better get those pumps started. Would you

mind?" Mother handed me to the principal and splashed her way out. He set me on a desk.

"How many polka dots are on my tie?" he asked.

I used my method for counting cereal boxes at the supermarket, the number up multiplied by the number sideways. Then I took some away because of the funny shape at the bottom of the necktie. "One hundred and fifty seven," I answered.

Principal DeGuy hopped onto the desk with me and emptied the water from his shoes. "Who is the queen of England?"

"I don't know."

"What is 157 multiplied by 23?"

I pushed the bangs out of my eyes. "3,611."

He ran the numbers. "Holy human calculator!"

The secretary handed him a telephone, and he dialed the number for the Office of Special and Gifted Testing. "Little lady," he told me, "if you are what I think you are, your whole world is about to change."

And, boy, did it ever. Not that I'm complaining. Once they found out my IQ was 204, they let me start school early. It was like a game to see how quickly I could pass each grade (fifth took only eight weeks and I skipped second, sixth, and tenth grades completely). But then, when I was eleven, they ran out of grades, so

I had to go away to college. Now I'm a thirteen-year-old graduate student at Harvard University.

At Harvard, everybody's brain is in overdrive all the time. So sometimes, when my brain is full of numbers and feels like it's going to explode, I slip away to an empty field on the edge of campus. Then I stretch out my arms and I spin.

2 Mindy Loft Tells It Like It Was

The reason I ramble is that I don't stay focused when I talk; at least that's what my eighth-grade English teacher told me at the beginning of this school year. So if I get a little off track, try not to get your poodle in a fluff. Anyway, if I had to pick, I'd say it all began the day that Miss Brenda shared her awful secret. I hadn't even met Aphrodite yet. I was thirteen years old and living with my mom in the apartment above her beauty shop, Tiffany's House of Beauty & Nails. We had a sign that Mom changed each week with stupid sayings like "Come on in and be a beauty, from your head to your patootie."

Mom made me help at the shop, doing gross stuff like sweeping piles of severed hair, boring stuff like re-filling the spray bottles, and a little bit of cool stuff like trying out the new nail polish. At least I got an allowance. But no matter how much I got paid, there was no way I was going to be a hairstylist for the rest of my life. My dream was to be a famous baton twirler.

When she was nineteen, my mom had been first runner-up for Miss Majorette of the Greater Allegheny Valley. My dad, John Loft (God rest his soul), had been one of the judges, and they had eloped before her trophy was back from the engraver. He became her manager, and they toured all over the country in a baby blue RV with a bumper sticker that said TWIRL TILL YOUR ARMS FALL OFF.

"With my panache and your talent, we're gonna set the world on fire," he told her, and they did.

Not the whole world, maybe, but at least part of the small town of Hermanfly, Nebraska. You see, there was this stupid Hermanfly Fourth of July Spectacular Parade. Dad was in a giant firecracker costume marching next to Mom, who was twirling a fire baton. They got too close and his fuse caught fire. Mom dropped the baton and screamed for help, and some woman in the crowd pulled a pair of scissors from her purse and clipped Dad's fuse just in time. That was the good news. The bad news was that by that time

Mom's flaming baton had rolled over to a storefront, which was where they were storing the fireworks for the big show.

Most everyone ran off as soon as the fireworks started going off, but Dad sat there in his firecracker costume holding onto Mom and staring up. He said that, next to Mom, it was the most beautiful thing he had ever seen. He was so pooped from all the excitement, Mom had to help him back to their motel.

The next morning, Dad was dead.

"Weak heart," the doctor told Mom. "Surprised he made it this long with that bum ticker."

Mom said a heart as big and kind as Dad's couldn't have been defective. She blamed the whole thing on the baton. So she quit the twirling circuit, moved back to Carnegie, Pennsylvania, and opened up a hair salon. That's when I was born. Because they reminded her of Dad, Mom still displayed her twirling awards all over the shop. My favorite thing to do when I was little was to pretend a hairbrush was a baton and strike poses like the figurines on top of the trophies.

One day, when I was four, I was doing a dance I made up and twirling a broken curling iron when Miss Brenda, the owner of Miss Brenda's Baton Barn, walked in the salon. She took one look at me and said, "Really, Tiffany, you can deny it all you want, but you know that little one has baton in her blood."

That creeped me out at first because I had just seen a cartoon with a vampire in it and I thought she said "bats in her blood." Even at four, I could be stupid like that. Anyway, I kept twirling whatever I could find (a customer's umbrella, another customer's walking cane, Mom's haircutting scissors) until Mom finally gave in and let me start taking lessons at Miss Brenda's Baton Barn. I still wasn't allowed to join the Squadettes (the lame name for the Baton Barn's competitive twirling team) because those twirlers had to march in the local parades. But Mom and Miss Brenda agreed that I could get unlimited private baton lessons in exchange for Miss Brenda getting unlimited salon services.

This was actually a good deal for Miss Brenda, whose mother had passed on great skin but whose father (who had to be part werewolf) had passed on a unibrow capable of growing so thick it looked like a caterpillar napping between her eyes. Miss Brenda would go to Tiffany's House of Beauty & Nails for eyebrow waxing, and, after it was gone, I would pretend it had turned into a butterfly and flown away. The day Miss Brenda shared her awful secret, it was sort of a medium larva.

That January morning, I rode my bike to Miss Brenda's Baton Barn for my private lesson. The studio was empty, and being the only twirler in that chilly space with its twenty-foot ceiling made me feel like the last Popsicle in the box. As soon as my hands thawed and we got started, I asked Miss Brenda to help me with a new trick I had been working on. She grabbed my baton, and it seemed to spin around her neck all on its own. Miss Brenda had this flow when she touched the baton, and a far-off look, like she was the bride and it was the groom and they were in love.

"You're so smooth," I said.

"Been doing this thirty-five years," said Miss Brenda. "Twirl in my sleep."

I pictured her baton whapping the ceiling with each throw as she snoozed. "Someday, I want to get as good as you," I said. I put the baton under my chin and used my neck to twirl it around my shoulders.

"You're something special, kiddo," said Miss Brenda. "With your natural flexibility and practice ethic, the sky's the limit." She gestured skyward and we both looked up. The baton I had gotten stuck in the rafters last week stared back at us. "Well, maybe not the sky. But at least the ceiling," she added. She was quiet for a moment, and when she spoke again her voice sounded, I don't know, heavier. Miss Brenda said, "There's something I need to tell you." She grabbed my baton mid-twirl. "I'm not supposed to say anything for another week, but, dang it, Mindy, I've known you since you were tiny, even taught your mom. I've got to give you a heads-up." She looked like she would burst into tears.

"Are you okay?" I asked. She led me to her "office," a desk in a supply closet. I followed her past the photographs on the hallway walls, including the newest one of last year's Squadettes holding up a small trophy. They were standing in front of a fence, smiling cluelessly while behind each girl's head metal things poked out like alien antennas. Looking at the team pictures made me feel left out sometimes, but there were lots of photos of me holding the trophies I'd won for my solo routines.

"I don't know how to break this to you, kiddo," Miss Brenda said as I sat on a box in her office, "but here goes. I'm selling out. Got an offer from the Cluck and Shuck chicken corn soup franchise for the land, enough for me to buy a condo in Florida. Baton is a young gal's sport. I've got no regrets. But at fifty-eight, it's time to face facts. A girl's gotta look out for herself.

I'll take you twirlers to the Twirlcrazy Grand Championship in May, but after that I'm through."

It felt like I'd been whacked in the gut with a 7/16-inch Fluted Super Star. "But Miss Brenda, you're the only baton studio in town, and, even if you weren't, there's no way we could afford to pay someone else for my lessons."

"Sorry, kiddo. I wish it didn't have to be this way."

"This can't be happening to me. What will I do if you close?"

"You'll land on your feet somehow." Then she must have said a bunch of other stuff to try to make me feel better, but I wasn't listening because I was thinking about how my life had been completely ruined. "Until I make an announcement," said Miss Brenda, "this is just between you and me. Right?"

She winked, and I gave her one of those pretend smiles we use in competitions, but inside I was ticked. Miss Brenda was wrong about me. I wasn't one of those girls who could land on her feet. I was good at only three things: being tall, being tanned, and being a twirler. And let's face it, being tall and having free use of Mom's tanning bed weren't things I could really take credit for. Twirling wasn't just an activity I did for fun like some of the Squadettes, who also took horseback riding lessons and ballet classes. Twirling was all I had.

When I was twirling, nobody called me stupid, snickered behind my back, or told dumb-blond jokes that they changed to dumb brown-haired to fit me. When I did a perfect split-leap pullout, not a single person in the audience cared what I scored on a standardized test, or that I had failed math my first semester of eighth grade and might get held back.

If the Baton Barn closed, my competitive twirling days would be over, and I'd be just another one of the dumb kids. Life was so unfair. Why did I always get the short end of the baton?

3   Aphrodite Describes Meeting Mindy for the First Time

If you're skinny and flat, like me, here's a fun thing you can do. Stand in front of a full-length mirror. Turn your body sideways. Now stick out your tongue. Behold! You're a zipper. I felt chipper as a zipper the morning I got dressed for my first day of teaching at Carnegie Middle School.

I wore the gray suit I used for presentations at Harvard, but tucked a pink silk handkerchief way down low in the front pocket of the jacket where nobody but I could see it. Even though my professors at Harvard discouraged me from wearing pink because it was "too little-girly" and "suggested a failure to appreciate the importance of a professional appearance," it was still my favorite color.

How did I make the transition from brilliant math

prodigy and Harvard graduate student to thirteen-year-old middle school remedial math teacher, you might be asking? More about that later. Suffice it to say that after my new-teacher orientation, I sat at the desk in front of my eighth-grade classroom waiting for the students to trickle in. I couldn't remember if I had been in the same classroom when I had attended Carnegie Middle School as a student, since I had passed through so quickly. Boring describes that room: naked bulletin board, crooked rows of wooden student desks, and dingy white walls. My gray suit sure didn't help to pep things up, so I pulled up the pink handkerchief till it peeked out of my breast pocket.

I knew it might feel a bit awkward at first teaching students who were the same age as me. However, I was confident that my air of authority and superior mathematical skills would make it impossible for any of the thirteen-year-old students in my class to think of me in any way other than as the distinguished educator I intended to be.

A boy wandered in and came over to my desk, leaning in close. He had a chubby face, yellow teeth, and the worst breath I had ever smelled. "Why are you sitting there?" he asked. He punctuated his consonants with big bursts of air. "Park your butt in the back."

Before I could think how to respond, Principal De-Guy came in. "That will be enough, Mr. Geruch."

Bad-breath boy backed off. "Anything you say, Mr. DeGuy."

Long-haired girls in wide-bottomed blue jeans and sparkly shirts wandered in, chatting and giggling. Noisy boys in straight-legged jeans and untied sneakers came in, punching one another's arms. I had memorized the seating chart, after one quick glance, so as soon as they were seated, I knew who they were. The last student to enter was the girl who had knocked me over in the stairwell earlier that morning. She gave me a suspicious look and took her seat. She was Mindy Loft. Her name suited her: she towered over me by at least a foot. She was a pretty girl, with sandy brown hair down to her waist, a slightly freckled complexion, and a strawberry scent.

Last, Miss Snipal blew in. Although she was the girls' gym teacher (and a former state Ping-Pong champion), Miss Snipal had been substituting as the math teacher. I was told the previous math teacher had quit the position in frustration because, despite her best effort, the remedial students "still couldn't tell an octagon from an octopus." I wasn't sure why the only substitute available was an expert at push-ups rather than add-ups, but I didn't want to seem nosy. I was just glad they were willing to hire me and give me a chance to teach. Principal DeGuy had asked Miss Snipal to join us as he introduced me to the class.

The bell rang, and my face heated. Since I'd turned thirteen, I had become more aware of my propensity to blush. It happened without warning, and at odd moments. I couldn't let the students see how nervous I was. Something that had always been stressed to me by my professors was that I should act my brain age, not my body age.

"Class," said Principal DeGuy, "it is my pleasure to introduce a remarkable young lady. Aphrodite Wigglesmith was four years old when I myself recognized her mathematical intellect. She graduated from elementary school at age eight, completed middle school the following year, and graduated from high school at age eleven."

The professors at Harvard called this the "dog and pony show." During the show, people would stare at me with widening mouths, and I would stare at something above their heads. They would see a petite girl, not especially pretty but no worse than plain-looking, slightly red in the face at the moment, with long bangs and dark shoulder-length hair pulled back efficiently with a barrette. I would see the dirty air vent, smudge, or similarly unremarkable feature on the spot of wall I was concentrating on. Today it was a spitball that had stuck and dried near the wall clock.

Principal DeGuy pulled a paper from his pocket and read: "After a perfect mathematics score on her SAT and a demonstration of substantial progress on the Millennium Prize Problems, Aphrodite Wigglesmith was admitted under special privilege to Harvard. She is the recipient of the Strangefellow Mathematics Award and the Fellowhood of the Traveling Calculator Prize. She was awarded a bachelor of science in mathematics from Harvard, and recently completed the requirements for a master's degree."

Principal DeGuy did not tell the class that while I was at Harvard I had to stay at the house of Harvard's dean of mathematical studies, Dr. Goode, instead of the dorm, and that my only real friend there had been a squirrel named Bernie, which I fed marshmallows and Tootsie Rolls. He also didn't tell how I came to be teaching remedial math to students in my hometown.

You see, I had a theory that nearly anyone could learn to be a math wiz—well, maybe not a total wiz, but at least wizish. Some students might take longer to understand a math concept than others, but their instruction could be tailored to suit their time:learning ratio.

Had I not been on my own individualized math path, I'd have never gotten this far. Why couldn't other students benefit from the same approach? The key would be a healthy dose of confidence to deter quitting. If other students believed in their potential as much as my teachers had believed in mine, why shouldn't they succeed?

To put it simply: E + C = MW (Effort + Confidence = Math Wiz).

In order to prove my theory, I needed to find a group of students who were as math challenged as possible. I'd sent out one hundred résumés to find a teaching job and received one hundred rejections. They all said the same thing: nobody would hire a thirteen-year-old math teacher. The solution to my problem came from a most unexpected place—a cafeteria bathroom.

"Somebody stop it!" yelled a Harvard freshman fleeing from a toilet that had begun spouting dirty water.

A pond formed around the stall and turned into a river.

"Ugh! Disgusting," said another girl as she, too, fled.

I watched the water approach. It reminded me of Carnegie Middle School and the man with the polka-dot tie, Principal DeGuy. *Could he use a mathematics teacher?* I wondered.

It was the second time a toilet changed my life.

So there I was, about to launch my teaching career in front of a class of thirteen-year-olds who had mostly flunked their first two quarters of math and would not be able to graduate and move on to high school unless I could turn them into math wizzes this spring.

"It is with great pleasure," said Principal DeGuy, "that I introduce your new teacher, Professor Aphrodite Wigglesmith."

Miss Snipal ceremoniously handed me a bucket of Ping-Pong balls. "If anybody gives you trouble," she said, "hit 'em with one of these."

Then Principal DeGuy and Miss Snipal left, and I was alone with seventeen math-challenged teenagers. I coughed. They stared. I cleared my throat. They stared. I removed from my book bag the index cards that I had prepared, and wrote my name on the board. Immediately, a hand shot up.

"I can't see it from here," said Salvador, a boy from the last row who wore thick, horn-rimmed glasses. "Can you put it higher?"

I erased my name. I had to stand on a nearby stool to get the wording high enough. It was an old metal stool, and when I stepped on it, the stool made a sound like an old woman passing wind. Students snickered and my face heated. I stretched my arm up to write high and the stool did it again. I wrote quickly and jumped off.

"Now the planets are in the way," said LeeAnn, a girl with enormous hoop earrings who sat on the left side of the second to last row. She pointed to a solar system mobile hanging from the ceiling.

I erased my name and tried to find a new spot to the right.

"Over a bit," said Roland.

"No, that's too far," said Keisha.

A couple of students snickered.

"Oh, knock it off," said Adam. "Stop picking on her."

"What do you expect?" asked a voice that had to belong to Hunter, who, sitting behind a student so much bigger than him, was almost completely concealed. "They send us a kid for a teacher. It's a joke."

The room exploded into a verbal riot.

"Give her a chance," said Adam. "She's got a degree from Harvard. Do you have any idea how hard it is to get into that school?"

"But look at her," said Mindy. "My aunt Peggy's Chihuahua is two inches taller."

"And probably smarter," added Roland. "I vote we give the job to the Chihuahua."

I should have been insulted, but I guess I was in shock. Most of the students in the back rows, led by Roland, openly opposed me. They sprang up and down in their seats and used animated hand gestures to emphasize their sincerity. A sprinkling of students, popping up like gophers in a field, led by Adam, defended me just as robustly. The students already sleeping at their desks showed no preference.

I turned to the chalkboard to figure where to print my name for maximum visibility. It's not that I wasn't stinging from the insults. It's just that I was a problem solver. I may not have been able to figure out how to look smarter than a Chihuahua, but I could use my math skills to try to solve the problem that had set the whole thing in motion. I examined the angles of unobstructed space to the board, and the objects that were in the way. Then I created an algebraic formula using those things as the variables. The chalk slapped against the board, leaving fragments. When I got to the second row of the formula, the class began to quiet. When I reached the end, the only sound was the chalk.

"Based upon my calculations, the best viewing area is here," I explained, drawing a line on the board and writing my name on it. My knees felt weak, but I kept my voice strong. "Any questions before I begin?"

Timothy raised his hand. "I have a question."

"Excellent." I said. "I would be happy to answer it."

"What does a mermaid wear to math class? An algebra. Get it?" He laughed. "Algae-bra."

The class groaned. I wanted to laugh, partly because I was still a little nervous and partly because I had never heard that math joke before, but I managed to control myself. Then I went into my prepared speech. "Mathematics," I said, "is one of mankind's most basic sources of knowledge. Many of the greatest problems of mankind have been solved through its use. Humans have literally moved mountains because of mathematics." They stared, as if momentarily fixed to their seats, and I continued. "Without it, there would be no bridges and no gasoline. Nobody could compensate for antigravity in outer space, or heat oil to the temperature that creates French fries. Without mathematics, life as we know it would cease to exist."

I wasn't sure if they were interested or getting ready for another attack. Somewhere I had read that a pack of wolves won't pounce on anything that is taller than it, so I picked up a math book, held it high, and continued.

"Mathematics is finite and infinite. It forces us

to ask why and how, which gives meaning and depth to our lives. It is the only learned discipline where one can achieve absolute truth."

They stared.

"We'll begin with an analysis of Lakatos's philosophy of mathematics." I lowered the book.

"All I want to know is enough to pass eighth grade," said Roland. "You ever teach fractions?"

"Well, no," I admitted.

"Square roots?"

"Actually, this will be the first time I've taught lower-grade math concepts."

Grumbling sounded across the classroom.

"I told you," said Roland. "They don't care about us. She doesn't know nothing about teaching."

"At least she knows more than you," said Adam.

Roland crumpled a paper from his notebook and threw it at Adam, who crumpled a paper and threw it at Roland in retaliation. Other students joined the fray, springing open their binders and using filler paper as ammunition. Mindy sat with her math book open, slowly ripping out pages and tearing them to shreds.

I thought about screaming, but I doubted anyone would hear me above the roar. Suddenly, Miss Snipal's Ping-Pong balls did not seem like such a bad idea.

"They're a rowdy bunch," Principal DeGuy had warned me. "Some real underachievers."

"Anyone can be a math wiz," I had assured him.

"Maybe," he said. "And maybe frogs can fly."

A giant spitball zipped by, inches from my head, and splattered onto the chalkboard. I ducked behind my desk for safety. It didn't matter to me if Principal DeGuy had his doubts, or even if my students did. I was going to prove that they could be math wizzes. I would instill confidence and inspire effort.

This class riot had not been part of my calculations, but I would not let it deter me. As soon as the students ran out of spitball ammunition, I would crawl out from under my desk and get to work.

4 Mindy Describes Meeting Aphrodite for the First Time

That's just like Aphrodite to totally forget how she bashed into me and almost killed me and to instead talk about the first day in her classroom. This is how we met: I was dumping stuff in my locker, and I was ticked because Mr. Green, my biology teacher, had just yelled at me for something I didn't do—my homework. Suddenly, some dumb book sailed over my head, crashed, and flopped down in front of me

"I've got it," this huge seventh grader cried as he scooped it up. He did a victory dance like a football player scoring a touchdown. "Oh, yeah."

Bobby DeGuy, the principal's son, rushed him. Even though he had gotten held back in third grade,

Bobby was still the smallest boy in the eighth grade, and whenever anyone wanted to play monkey in the middle, Bobby was always the monkey. "Give it back— or else," he said.

"Whatcha gonna do?" the bigger boy teased. "Tell Daddy?" He sent the book sailing to another boy, whose left hook sent it crashing into the locker right at my feet.

If it had been something important to me at the time, I might have picked it up—but it was just a stupid math book, so I stepped over it and kept walking. I had a bigger concern, a chipped nail, and not just a chip in the glittery peach polish. The nail tip was a complete jagged mess. Naturally, I headed for the bathroom.

If I'm going to be late for class, I thought, *I might as well take my time.* I used an emery board to smooth and shape it, and touched up the edge with my spare polish. The girls in my class always made a fuss about my nails being long and fancy, but they had no idea what a giant pain it was to keep them looking good. Since I never knew when Mom might ask me to help with a manicure customer, I was pretty much stuck keeping them "perfect" all the time. Miss Brenda said I should get extra points when I competed for not whacking them off with my baton. I pulled out the novelty folding baton I kept in my backpack and gave it a few spins, using the breeze to dry the nails, before checking my face in the mirror.

For my thirteenth birthday, Mom had bought me a makeup kit the size of Montana. She said applying blush under the cheekbones would make my face look thinner and using mascara would make my eyes look larger. Grandma Lucy always says you shouldn't judge a cover by its book, or was it a book by its cover? Anyway, Mom disagreed.

"Beauty is the family business," Mom had explained to me. "When you look bad, Tiffany's House of Beauty and Nails looks bad."

Beauty was easy for Mom because she had wavy auburn hair and was naturally glamorous. Even her name, Tiffany, was pretty. What kind of a boring name is Mindy? In addition to a totally dumb name, I got stuck with boring brown hair I have to wash every day, and, even worse, a nose that breaks out in stupid freckles if I forget to wear concealer and sunblock. No matter what you look like, Mom tells her customers, the trick is to act like you're pretty. If you think you are, you will be. So even though I felt like a total fake sometimes, that's what I tried to do.

I changed my eyelids from lilac to blue and rubbed strawberry lotion into my hands. I bent down, tossing my long hair over my head, and brushed fifty times. By the time I checked my watch, class was half over and, really, it's better not to go at all when you're that late. So I grabbed a fashion magazine from my backpack and read "How to Eat Yourself Slim with Chocolate Cupcakes." When the bell rang, I hurried to my next class. I could always make up an excuse why I missed one class, but missing more and getting away with it was harder. I stormed up the crowded steps when—

Crash!

I fell against the kids behind me like some dumb domino. My backpack went flying, and a foot smashed my hand. A shrimpy girl with black hair wearing a gray suit sprawled next to me. She pushed her bangs out of the way and rubbed a red spot on her forehead. The crowd kept coming, and kids stepped over us, complaining we were blocking the way.

"Omigosh!" said Timothy. He grabbed me by the arm to help me up. Timothy has had a "secret" crush on me since I was six, and for once I was grateful he followed me around. The boy who sometimes followed Timothy grabbed my other arm. "Are you all right?"

"That girl slammed into me," I told them. "She didn't even say sorry. She just sat there as if she's never been knocked down before."

Like that wasn't bad enough, then Principal DeGuy came rushing down the stairs two steps at a time to help the girl up. "Holy tumbleweeds! So sorry, Aphrodite. These stairwells can be dangerous with the students charging up and down. Let's go to my office."

Of course, I had no idea at the time that the rag doll with the skinny limbs who Principal DeGuy was leading down the steps was my new math teacher. I figured she was just some dumb new kid. I even stuck my tongue out at her as she passed, although she didn't seem to notice.

"I'm okay, too," I said to Principal DeGuy's back. "Thanks for asking."

"You stampeding elephants should get to class," he shouted, before dragging the girl out of view.

The rest of the crowd took his advice and rushed off, leaving me and Timothy alone. I plopped down on a step and reached for my backpack. Something was oozing from the front pocket. My tube of strawberry hand lotion must have exploded when it hit the ground.

"Ugghhh!" I pulled out a tissue and began wiping off the mess. My hand was still throbbing from the fall, and the nail I had fixed was totally snapped in half.

"Looks like you're in a jam," said Timothy. "A strawberry jam. Get it?" (Did I mention he had an annoying habit of telling incredibly lame jokes?)

"Oh, can it," I replied.

And that's how I met Aphrodite.

5   Aphrodite Ducks Squash

If you are ever on the receiving end of flying squash, do this. First, remain seated. Standing will just make you a bigger target. Second, dart your head to the left or right, but never duck. The curvature of the spoon tends to fling the squash low, so you will take it in the head if you duck. Third, try to remember that it's only squash, and it washes off with water.

That evening, the mashed squash hit my left eyebrow. "No, no," I told my baby brother, Hermy, the food-flinging fanatic. "In the cave. Put the yummy in the cave. Just like me." I demonstrated by scooping up a spoonful of peas, dumping them in my mouth, and chewing with exaggerated satisfaction.

Hermy pointed to his own mouth. "Cave," he squealed.

I wiped off the squash. Dinners had lost all civility since my baby brother joined us at the table, and I couldn't have been happier. Hermy never criticized me for baby talk or acting silly. It's not that I didn't love my parents, but, like my professors, they made me feel like I had to act mature. My mother was an especially serious person. If she were a drink, it would be water. My father, Buster Wigglesmith, would be a cup of warm milk. Hermy would be a fizzy cherry soda with a scoop of piña colada ice cream and a slice of lime served in a Winnie-the-Pooh glass.

Hermy was twenty-one months old. He was born while I was at Harvard. My father, a mythology buff, named him Hermes after the Greek god who bridged the mortal and immortal worlds, just as he had named me Aphrodite after the Greek goddess of love and beauty. Hermy had a quick smile, and passed gas when he laughed too hard. His chubby face reminded me of the dolls that my grandmother gave me before my math professors said they would distract me from my intellectual development.

I loved Hermy's free spirit. When he colored outside the lines, I rewarded him with cookies. When he "shared" his pacifier with the neighbor's dog and the dog swallowed it, I bought him a dozen replacement pacifiers. A few months ago, I moved out of the sunny bedroom and into the smaller bedroom at the end of the hall because Hermy liked the morning sun on his face.

The doctors had started to chart Hermy's development to see if he would be a genius, too. Most everyone seemed disappointed when he turned out to be normal. I was relieved for him, because it meant he wouldn't have to give up things like coloring outside the lines and flinging squash.

My mother passed the dinner rolls to my father. I licked my spoon and pressed it onto my nose. Hermy laughed so hard squash came out of his nostrils.

"Is that how you behaved at Harvard?" Mother asked.

"Of course not," I said. "Harvard is a serious place."

Hermy dumped his bowl of squash over his head. Streams of thick orange paste ran down his face.

"Where's the camera?" I asked my father. He was naturally laid back and took Hermy's shenanigans in stride. He liked to say he didn't need to worry about anything because Mother worried for them both. My father had been the original plumber in the family, and my mother his appointment- and bookkeeper. When he broke his leg changing a stranger's flat tire and couldn't take on plumbing jobs, Father took it in stride. "Life is what you make it," he said. Sure enough, it turned out that Mother was better at plumbing and Father was better at staying home and keeping the books, so they switched jobs and that's the way it's been ever since.

Father chuckled at Hermy's pumpkin face and went to find the camera for me. I took a snapshot of Hermy with the bowl on his head. Then another of him after he took the bowl off and began shampooing the gooey squash into his hair. Hermy washed his face with his sticky squash hands, mugging for the camera. "Dytee!" he squealed.

"Don't encourage him," Mother said as I snapped away.

Father leaned back in his chair. "Lighten up a bit, honey. It's normal for a baby to play with his food."

"Aphrodite never did," Mother replied.

"But she was never . . ." Father's voice trailed off, but I knew what he was going to say.

"Normal," I added, putting the camera down.

The word hung in the air. Part of me liked being a child prodigy. But another part of me didn't enjoy feeling like I was different all the time. I knew that I was lucky to be able to get a college degree when I was so young, but I didn't feel lucky while surrounded by Harvard students twice my age and size who always got quiet when I entered the room, as if they couldn't be themselves when they were around me. Real luck, it seemed to me, was what Hermy had: a body and a brain that matched.

After dinner, I went to my room and took out my neon-pink diary. I used it to record ideas regarding my theory that anyone could be a math wiz. Once my research at Carnegie Middle School was completed and I'd proved my theory, the plan was for me to move back to Boston and take a job teaching at Harvard. That's where my professors said my math talent could best be used.

I put on my pink-polka-dot pajamas and reached for Hershey Bear. My mother had won him at an amusement park on my fourth birthday. The man in the red cap tried to guess my mother's age. He said she was twenty-nine, even though she was only twenty-five, so I won a prize. That was my best birthday. It was before Principal DeGuy made me take the IQ test and everyone treated me like I was different. Hershey Bear was hot-chocolate brown and marshmallow soft, and I slept with him every night. Not that I could admit such a thing and expect people to take me seriously.

"But look at her," Mindy had said. "My aunt Peggy's Chihuahua is two inches taller."

"And probably smarter," Roland had added. "I vote we give the job to the Chihuahua."

It was mean, and I should have been angry. But in my heart, I could understand their reservations. How could a thirteen-year-old teacher expect her thirteen-year-old students to take her seriously? Because of my age and small stature, I would have to work hard to prove myself to my class. My students would not show me respect until I earned it. There was nothing I could do about my physical appearance, but I could try to win them over with my intellectual prowess. I would impress them with my ability to solve complicated equations. That should do the trick.

6 Mindy Ducks Aphrodite

When you really think about it, math is like a foreign language, and I'm not bilingual, so it's not my fault that I stink at it. After two weeks of Professor Wigglesmith's lectures, I was in a total fog. You know that movie Invasion of the Zombie Snatchers, the part at the end where there's just that one zombie left and she's wandering around the cemetery in a daze? That was me in Professor Wigglesmith's math class. She drew fancy stuff on the board and spoke about the heart and soul of mathematics, while I daydreamed about one of the zombie killers surviving so I could be put out of my misery.

It might not have been so bad if Veronica, Summer, Jordeen, or one of my other friends was in remedial math with me so we could pass notes or something, but the rest of the kids in bonehead math were mostly nerds and misfits. They tuned out, too, but in their own ways, reading manga or hooking up to MP3s, which Professor Wigglesmith never even noticed. Although we weren't learning, nobody complained. It was better than getting hit by Ping-Pong balls, like when Miss Snipal was in charge. Being in Miss Snipal's class had been like living in a Three Stooges movie—one dumb move and you got whacked.

When Miss Snipal first set her red bucket full of Ping-Pong balls on the desk, I thought we were going to play some kind of game. "Can I ask a question?" I said. It's one of my stupid habits—asking if I can ask a question before I ask a question.

Miss Snipal threw a Ping-Pong ball, and it just missed my cheek. "Raise your hand if you want to talk," she said. "Better yet, don't talk. Just listen. I will be your substitute from now on. If a team is losing, they send in a new coach. You are a losing team, and you should be grateful that I volunteered to whip you into shape until a permanent teacher can be found."

Eugenia raised her hand. She was a shy girl whose idea of a social life was cleaning out her hamster's cage on a Saturday night. Eugenia wore the same black sweater every day, but it was so clean she either washed it every evening or had a whole row of them lined up in her closet. I imagined her getting up in the morning and dressing her hamster in an identical sweater. Anyway, Eugenia said, "I don't mean to be rude, Miss Snipal, but I don't think I belong in remedial math. Isn't there room in the academic math class for me?"

A ball hit her in the nose.

"Stop whining," Miss Snipal said. "If your name is on my roster, you belong here. If you want out, you need to work harder. Push yourself. Feel the burn. Here's the game plan: we'll start with five repetitions of multiplication tables, and then do a few sets of counting by odd and even numbers. If we have time, we'll squeeze in counting backwards by root numbers. Any questions?" The only sound was that of the balls rubbing together in her hands.

Asking a gym teacher to teach math is like asking a French teacher to give scuba-diving lessons. After two semesters of Miss Snipal, practically the whole class was drowning. I would never have believed that anyone could be a worse math teacher than Miss Snipal, until I met Aphrodite Wigglesmith.

After two weeks of staring at Professor Wigglesmith's back as she filled the board with numbers, things were more hopeless than ever. Even if I hadn't ripped up half the pages in my book, math was too hard.

Then there she was, Professor Wigglesmith, coming down the school hallway toward me. And there I was—ducking into the bathroom to avoid her. I hadn't planned to cut class, but with Miss Genius in charge, I was on my way to flunking out anyway. So what difference did it make?

I threw my backpack onto the sink and pulled out my baton for practice. But twirling just reminded me about how the Baton Barn was going to be bought by the Cluck and Shuck people. I imagined my baton falling from the rafters one day and whapping a customer right in his chicken corn soup. Even that didn't make me feel better.

I closed my eyes and tried to conjure up my favorite daydream—Adam Boyce sitting in the front row at one of my baton competitions. Adam was without question the hottest boy in the eighth grade. Broad shoulders? Check. Blond hair that he gelled into tiny spikes? Check. Total MVP on both the wrestling team and basketball team? Check. Check. There wasn't a girl in the class who didn't have a crush on Adam, even if he did act like he didn't notice. Maybe it was the fact that he didn't notice that made me like him more. I mean, even with my straight brown hair and stupid freckled nose, there were still lots of boys who wanted to be seen with me. But in the world of middle school dating, Adam was like the big trophy a girl got when she came in first place.

In my daydream, he was gawking at me like I was the only girl in the world, and in my sparkling gold dance outfit, I was. I soared onto the stage, batons dancing on my fingertips. I threw them high in the air, did a cartwheel, caught them in perfect unison, and went into a split.

"Min-dy. Min-dy . . . ," the crowd began to chant. The faster I spun, the louder they chanted. "Min-dy. Min-dy. . . ."

Someone was shaking my arm.

"Mindy? What are you doing?" It was Professor Wigglesmith. I hadn't noticed her come in. I was sitting on the floor under a sink, and my head was resting against a plumbing pipe like it was a pillow. I must have dreamed the whole period away.

"I don't feel well," I said. "I guess I'm sick."

"So that's why you missed class," Professor Wigglesmith guessed.

I got up, splashed my face, patted it dry with a paper towel, and unzipped my makeup bag. Two girls walked in. One went into a stall and the other asked to borrow my lipstick. After they left, I noticed that Professor Wigglesmith was watching me put on mascara.

"Doesn't that make you tear?" she asked.

"You get used to it," I said. Through the mirror, I looked over at Professor Wigglesmith. Her face was so pale next to her charcoal turtleneck it looked almost featureless. I felt a little sorry for her. "You could use some color." I dug out my new lipstick and held it out like one of the Sioux Indians we learned about in social studies might offer a peace pipe to a member of the Iroquois tribe. "Do you want to try some?"

7 Aphrodite Glues Them to Their Seats

Here's some more advice. If a girl ever offers to share her lipstick with you, do not hesitate; grab it and start puckering. Above all, don't do what I did. The lipstick was passion pink, and just the thought of trying it made my lips tingle. But, as a teacher, I was supposed to be educating students, not sharing lipstick, even if it was passion pink. I tried to think of something educational. Finally, I replied, "There are millions of germs in the human mouth. Even if only one-tenth come into contact with the lips, there could be tens of thousands of germs living on that lipstick."

Mindy dumped the lipstick into her makeup bag. "What kind of a mean thing is that to say?"

"But it's true."

"That doesn't mean you should say it." She folded her arms. "How would you like it if I told *you* the truth?"

I sensed there was something Mindy wanted to say, a secret of some sort that she wanted to share with me. Perhaps something personal that had been bothering her. "I'm sure I'd like it very much," I answered.

"Are you making fun of me?" she asked. "Because if you are, it'll be the camel that breaks the straw's back."

"I think you mean the straw that breaks the camel's back."

"There you go again, acting like you know everything. You want the truth?"

I assumed it was a rhetorical question, but she waited as if I was to answer. With Mindy misinterpreting everything I said, and with her towering over me, grim-faced and arms folded, the best I could do was nod apprehensively.

"You asked for it," she said. "So here it comes: the whole class is probably failing because none of us can understand what you keep talking about."

I felt like a tiny mouse standing under the proverbial camel as it collapsed.

"You may be a genius," Mindy continued, so agitated her voice rose an octave, "but you're the worst math teacher ever. I'm not sick. I cut math class because it's a waste of time. I don't know how to add fractions. I can't tell a number line from a clothesline, or a square root from a hair root." She threw her backpack over her shoulder. "If I don't learn something soon, I'm going to fail math and have to repeat eighth grade. Do you have any idea how totally humiliating that would be?" She took one final look in the mirror, said, "Oh, what's the use?" and stomped off.

That night, I kept replaying the scene in my mind. I set Hershey Bear on my nightstand. "Do you think I've been teaching over their heads, too?" I asked rhetorically. He fell forward and landed with one paw up in the air as if in agreement. I returned him to the nightstand with a sigh. "I've been so focused on showing off my math skills that I'm afraid I haven't been a very good teacher. Instead of earning their respect, I've bored them into such a stupor they don't have the energy to complain. I'll never prove my theory that way. I suppose the best thing to do would be to have a long talk with my students about how to change the situation." Hershey Bear fell again, tumbling with his caboose in the air. "If I can't even get you to sit still while I talk, how will I ever get the class to listen?"

I thought about my first day of teaching middle school, how I had lost control of the class and it had descended into chaos. I could still see the students springing up and down in their seats as I dodged giant spitballs. If I could just find a way to keep their glutei maximi glued to their seats and maintain order, maybe I could explain my mistake and get a second chance.

The next day, as soon as my class was seated, two students got out playing cards. Three others held small video games on their laps. None of them even looked in my direction. How could I not have noticed before their complete lack of interest?

"Today," I told the students, "we'll be trying something different."

The only reply was the ticking clock.

"I'm going to make a list of what it is that you want me to teach." A few looked up, but the rest acted as if deaf. "Who would like to go first?"

Nobody responded. I glanced at Mindy. She was slouched in her seat with her head behind her math book.

"Mindy?" She lowered her head into her book. My cheeks burned. How could I prove my theory that anyone could learn to be a math wiz when I couldn't even get a student to look at me? I forced my voice to sound strong. "I know you can hear me."

Mindy slammed her book closed and tossed it in her backpack.

"What are you doing?"

She headed for the door.

"Where are you going?"

"To the principal's office. I figured I might as well save you the trouble of sending me."

"Why?" I asked.

"Aren't you giving me detention for yesterday?"

"Detention?" I almost laughed. "I should give you a medal. That was the smartest thing anyone ever said to me."

Her face went blank.

"Seriously," I added.

The whole class stared as Mindy slipped back into her seat.

"Logic dictates that when an approach to a problem doesn't work, it should be abandoned." Then I realized I was doing it, explaining things in a way that wasn't getting through. "We've gotten off to a bad start, and I'd like to begin again. But this time, I'd like you to tell me what math concepts you want to learn."

"You're asking us what to teach?" said Roland.

I nodded, and the room fell quiet for what felt like a millennium. Finally, Roland folded his arms and pursed his lips. "Fractions," he said. "Multiplying and dividing them."

I wrote the word *fractions*, being careful to continue facing the class so I could tell if anyone was losing interest. "What else?"

It was like I had turned on a faucet. First their requests came in drips, then streams, and then a torrent: fractions and decimals, ratios, positive and negative numbers, square roots, number lines, orders of operation, and perimeters and circumferences. By the end of the class, the lower section of the blackboard was covered, and I had to drag the stool over to add things on top. The stool tooted away, but the students were so busy yelling out things for me to add they acted like they didn't hear it. Finally, I jumped down.

"Professor Wigglesmith?" It was Eugenia. She lowered her hand. "Isn't that an awful lot of things to learn? I mean, for us you-know-whats?"

"She means boneheads," Mindy said. "That's what they call us."

"Who calls you that?" I asked.

"Everyone," said Roland.

I'd never even heard the expression before. "Why?"

"Because we're stupid," said Roland. "This class will never learn all that stuff. Not the morons you have in here." To illustrate his point, he scratched his head with his right hand and under his arm with his left while making monkey sounds. A couple of the other students made jungle noises, too, apparently to demonstrate their agreement.

"Shut up," Adam yelled. "Some of us *want* to pass this class."

Mindy ripped a page out of her math book, crinkled it into a ball, and threw it at Roland. "Yeah, keep your mouth shut. Some of us *need* to pass this class."

Roland blew bad breath in her direction. "What you gonna do about it? Hit me with a pom-pom?"

"Twirlers don't use pom-poms, you idiot. We use batons."

While students insulted one another, I erased the board and, in the precise spot I knew was best, wrote "11." Then I waited for silence. "Who knows what this is?" I asked.

"We're dumb, but we're not that dumb," said Salvador, adjusting his glasses. "It's the number eleven. So what?"

"Eleven is how old Winston Churchill was when he

failed sixth grade. Did he give up on himself? No. He went on to become a great leader and the prime minister of the United Kingdom." Then I wrote "10" on the board. "In tenth grade, Michael Jordan is reputed to have failed to win a spot on his high school's basketball team. Did he question his athletic ability and accept failure? He wouldn't have become the greatest basketball player of all time if he had. The history and record books are full of people whose ability in their youth was doubted. They had to believe in themselves to succeed."

I clapped the chalk dust off my hand, satisfied, and the bell rang. Roland was the first to move. His chair lifted off the ground with him. The other students also tried to get up, but their chairs were glued to their butts as well.

"I took the liberty," I explained, "of applying special temporary glue to your chairs before class began."

"You did what?" asked Salvador, pushing against his chair in vain.

"I wanted to make sure you would sit and listen to me. But there's no cause for concern. The glue lasts only fifty minutes." I checked my watch. "It should wear off in twenty-three seconds."

The scene dissolved into a twisted version of musical chairs as students hopped around with chairs stuck to their rears.

"It's not coming off," LeeAnn complained.

I counted down. "Sixteen seconds, fifteen seconds."

"This is ridiculous," Hunter said, searching his overstuffed backpack for something to pry loose his seat.

"Twelve seconds, eleven seconds."

Mindy was the only student who could stand. She looked confused.

"I didn't think it necessary to get your attention," I told her.

"No fair," said Keisha as she tried to wrench the chair from Eugenia's tush.

I expected Mindy to be pleased, but she just shook her head and left. "Five, four, three, two, one."

As we waited for the chairs to drop, the room fell silent. The late bell rang and the room erupted in complaints again. It was then that I checked the glue bottle and realized I had misread the glue's holding time. It was five hundred minutes.

8 Mindy Wows Them in the Alley

A lot of the kids were totally ticked about having chairs stuck to their butts at first, but then word spread and everyone was talking about it and they were like celebrities. It helped that the glue was just stuck to their clothes and not their skin so they could hop to the bathroom, squirm out, and change into clothes from the Lost and Found. When Principal DeGuy found out what had happened, he said it was an "innovative teaching strategy" and called Professor Wigglesmith brilliant. Can you believe that? I would have been in detention for a month if I had pulled a "brilliant" stunt like that.

The next day, in math class, Professor Wigglesmith promised not to do it again and said she hoped we could put the incident "behind" us, but among the students you could tell something had changed. There's a kind of weird respect you get for pranking, and we all realized we had witnessed the most awesome teacher prank ever at Carnegie Middle School. It may sound dumb, but knowing your teacher could spring such a trick made class more exciting. What could be next?

Professor Wigglesmith started giving us daily pep talks. She said, "We are all born with intelligence, but use only a small fraction of our potential. That means some of it is sitting there going to waste. All you have to do is use it." Then she wrote the symbol for infinity. "This is what you are—potential," she told us. "Not boneheads. From now on, you should treat yourselves, and one another, with respect for your potential."

That was the day she gave out the honorary degrees. Maybe it was because she had just made a mistake in front of all of us, or maybe it was something she had planned all along, but she pulled out a stack of fake "diplomas" and made each one of us come up. Then she read a bunch of gobbledygook that I think was Latin. She said that since she had just as much to learn as we did, from now on she was going to call each of us professor, too.

"What am I a professor of?" I asked as she handed me a scroll.

She said, "You are a Professor of Unlimited Potential, Professor Loft."

You could tell that most of the kids thought it was really cool, and right away they started calling one another Professor this and Professor that, but I wasn't sure what to make of it. In my whole life, nobody had ever called me smart. Let's face it; some girls are not destined to be rocket scientists. I was descended from a particularly long line of total scatterbrains.

"If my eyes weren't glued to their sockets, I'd forget where I left them," my grandma Lucy always says. Once she volunteered to help decorate my elementary school for a reading festival. She was in charge of hanging pictures of fictional characters in the cafeteria, but instead of using removable tape, she used superglue, so when the festival was over, the parts where she had used the most glue wouldn't come off. Even today, you still can see the Cat in the Hat's head hanging over the salad bar, the Queen of Hearts' left arm near the juice machine, and Wilbur the Pig's rump over the cashier station.

And Grandma Lucy's reputation was nothing compared to my mom's, whose mix-ups are really legend. Once Mom needed to buy new hair rollers for the beauty shop, so she went onto eBay and bid on what she thought was a lot of 1,200 French curlers but was actually 1,200

French crullers. Turns out, a cruller is a type of doughnut. A week later, a bakery truck appeared with one hundred boxes of them. Do you know how hard it is to use up 1,200 doughnuts? We gave a free doughnut away for every inch of hair cut and every fingernail painted. We even strung them on a line and hung them on a sign that said: "If your hair is in a rut, try our homemade shampoo à la doughnut." Then someone called the Department of Health on us and the police came and took all the doughnuts and we never saw the police or the doughnuts again. Even today, when people in town do something stupid you can sometimes hear them say they're having a "doughnut moment" in honor of my mom.

Anyway, to make a short story long, after I confronted her in the bathroom and she decided to pay more attention to teaching us the basics, Professor Wigglesmith went into overdrive with her lesson plans. On Mondays, she would teach a concept, and the next day we would do reinforcement exercises. On Wednesdays, she would give a pretest, and on Thursdays the students who had scored highest on the pretest would be assigned as "peer mentors" to help the others. Friday would be another test, and the Student-Teacher of the Week would win a free homework pass.

Students who didn't get a least a C on the test would be put on a list for home tutoring, which Professor Wigglesmith herself would do. Three weeks passed, and a lot of the kids were bragging about how their stupid grades were improving and how the system seemed to be working. But when I checked the home tutoring list, my name appeared again for the third week in a row.

That evening, my plan was to zip through my dumb science homework fast as I could. I would leave math for last, since Professor Wigglesmith was coming over at 7:30 p.m. to torture—I mean tutor—me. At 7:15, the doorbell buzzed like someone was holding it down. I thought it was rude of Professor Wigglesmith to lean on it and I was going to tell her, so I flung open the door.

"Hey, girl," Veronica, Jordeen, and Summer chirped in unison. The three had been my closest friends since forever, and were so inseparable that people often called them "The VJs." When we hung out, people called us "VJs & M," sort of like "PB & J."

"Our moms are getting their nails done and they gave us twenty bucks to get lost," Summer said. "You want to hang out? They changed the display at the Shoe Palace. You know what that means."

"New shoes!" the other girls chimed.

"I am so totally with you," I told them. I was grabbing my coat when I saw it: my math book. I felt so low, I practically crawled to the door. "I can't. Miss Math Genius is coming to tutor me."

"I'm so glad I'm not a bonehead like you," said Veronica.

I almost said we don't call one another boneheads anymore, but then I remembered that was just in Professor Wigglesmith's class. To the rest of the school we were still boneheads. When my friends made a comment about my crappy grades, I always pretended it was funny and laughed about it. That way they wouldn't know it bothered me.

"It's bad enough you have to take remedial math," Veronica continued, "but to have to take it with that nerd teaching! She's so lame."

"Ditto," said Summer. "I've heard her talking when I walk past her classroom. She's always 'infinity this' and 'potential that.' And every time she climbs on that stool, she farts."

I wanted to tell Summer that the stool only makes that sound because Roland took out a couple of screws and slipped in a whoopee cushion to mess with her, like he does for all the substitutes, but I didn't want them to think I was trying to defend Professor Wigglesmith.

Veronica flipped a strand of her copper-highlighted hair and laughed. "Plus she's got a funny voice, like, I don't know, tin or something. And she's so stiff about things—"

"Wait. I can do an impression of her," said Jordeen. "Okay, I'm Wigglesmith on a date." She made her voice sound like a robot. "Excuse me, young man. It would give me pleasure if you would relocate the fleshy folds surrounding your mouth to the fleshy folds surrounding my mouth."

It sounded so much like the kind of clueless thing Professor Wigglesmith might actually say, I laughed a little even though it felt wrong.

"Like Wigglesmith would ever have a date," said Veronica. "Who would want to get close to that weirdo?"

"Excuse me," said a soft voice. "I have a 7:30 appointment with Professor Loft." Professor Wigglesmith stepped forward. She was wearing dark pink pants and a pastel pink jacket, and was carrying a bulging black leather briefcase.

Veronica, Summer, and Jordeen turned and clomped down the steps before I could even think of a way to explain the "Professor Loft" thing without it sounding stupid. I wasn't sure if Professor Wigglesmith's face had turned pink because she had overheard us or if it was just part of her monochromatic outfit.

After the girls left and Professor Wigglesmith and I got settled inside, Mom brought a tray of tea and cookies into the living room. I picked up a chocolate chip cookie and nibbled around the edges, trying my best not to notice that Professor Wigglesmith looked like the victim of an explosion at a pink paint factory. It was strange, because when she taught she wore gray suits all the time. Now here she was in a getup that made her look like a giant pink hot dog waiting for a bun. You'd think she'd know better than to dress like Oscar Mayer when she's trying to get a bonehead—I mean "Professor Bonehead"—like me to take her seriously.

"No offense," I said, "but can I ask you a question? I mean, do you think you look good in that outfit?"

She examined her clothes like she was looking for a stain.

I rolled my eyes. "I mean, the whole thing is just so . . . so . . . pink."

"It's my favorite color," she explained.

"That doesn't mean you need to wrap yourself in it from head to toe. You look like a piece of bubblegum stuck in a cotton candy machine."

She gave me one of those polite half smiles that

aren't really smiles at all, and I felt a little bad about leveling with her. That's when I noticed I was wearing a blue T-shirt with my blue jeans. Of course, in my case, the single-color thing was just a coincidence. I didn't know how to explain why it looked cool when I did it by accident but weird when she did it on purpose, so I decided to ask her another question. I picked at my cookie. "So, do you really believe that stuff about none of us being dumb?"

"Why else would I say it?" She broke her cookie into four equal bites. "I've looked at your tests. The longer you do a particular type of problem, the more you get wrong."

"So I *am* stupid."

"No. Making mistakes doesn't mean you're stupid. It means you're human."

"Then why have I been failing?"

"Students who second-guess themselves often get the right answer but erase it because they don't trust themselves. I've seen a lot of that on your papers. Plus, your fundamentals are a bit rusty, but that's something we can work on. The real focus in secondary mathematics these days is not on memorizing formulas or facts. It's on nurturing a deeper understanding. You're best at word problems, and that's meaningful because word problems require one to delve deeper into the central mathematical concept being explored."

"Um, could you translate that for me?" I asked.

"Sorry," she said. "It just means word problems can be tricky, but you have a knack."

"A knack, huh?" She looked totally serious when she said it, like she wasn't just pretending so she could turn around and make fun of me. It made me feel I was special when she said it, like the way I felt when I pulled off a perfect routine and won a trophy, and that gave me an idea. I stuffed the last of the cookie into my mouth. "There is *something* that I know I'm good at. Want to see?"

I led her down the steps and through the beauty salon, grabbed a baton, and slipped out the back door. The alley was just a dump, but I liked it for baton practice because there were only nine feet between the buildings, making it easier to tell if my baton was flying straight when I threw it. The smell in the alley was a combination of peanut shells from the Irish pub across the way, used animal litter from Sid's Pet-O-Rama a few doors down, and whatever else happened to be in the Dumpster. I was afraid Professor Wigglesmith might say something mean about it, but she said the alley smelled like her baby brother.

I had her stand against the wall and started doing my routine from when I'd won second place at the Mid-Atlantic Junior Twirl Finals. I threw the baton up, spun three times, and caught it with the hand behind my back. That opening always got the crowd excited. Then I did some rolls and aerials, all while dancing and tumbling to the routine's theme song in my head, "I'm Walking on Sunshine." I wasn't sure I would get the timing right without my music, but by the time I got to the end, I hadn't made a single drop. I did a double walkover, threw the baton all the way to the third story, did another double walkover, then stretched out my right hand and closed my eyes. The baton landed in my palm. I flung it across my chest and bowed. "So? What do you think?" I asked.

Professor Wigglesmith clapped so hard I thought she might hurt herself. Then she walked around me staring up and down at the walls, as if calculating their height. "How did you know the baton would land in your hand without looking?"

"Practice," I said, twirling from hand to hand. "It's easy to do tricks if you practice every day. I've been practicing my throws in this alley two hours a day since I was six." Out of habit, I twirled as we talked.

Whenever I held the baton, it felt like it should be in motion.

"If you can get that good at baton through practice," she said, "you can be a math wiz. Math and baton aren't that different. They both require dedication and hard work. Might I try?"

I handed her the baton, and she examined it like it was an alien. "Turn up, turn under, like this," I said, showing her how to do a simple twirl.

She tried to mimic, but the baton clunked against her elbow. I showed her again, and this time she managed not to whack herself too bad. She had this droopy elbow thing going on, but once we fixed that she actually got it going a bit. It felt cool to be the teacher for a change. I went inside to get another baton so we could twirl together. I came out just as Professor Wigglesmith spread her legs out for balance, lowered the baton, and flung it in the air. It flew crooked, crashed into a window, and broken glass rained down. The baton hit the pavement on the ball end and bounced up.

"Omigosh! You broke my window!"

"I forgot to take into account the difference in our arm strengths—and that I haven't developed the ability to throw it straight," she said.

"You forgot to take into account that my mom is going to kill me," I replied.

Professor Wigglesmith reached into the pocket of her jacket and fished out a wad of cash. She peeled off two one-hundred-dollar bills and handed them to me. "Do you think that's enough to cover the cost?"

"What are you, rich or something?"

She shrugged. "Every time I win a math contest, I get a prize. Plus, now I get money for teaching at the middle school. My parents have asked me to stop buying them things, and Hermy already has every toy in the store. I don't have anything else to spend it on, so I always have a lot of ready cash."

I held a bill up close for inspection, in case she was trying to pull something on me. The name under the picture said FRANKLIN. The only hundred-dollar bill I had held before was beige and printed with the word MONOPOLY. "How do I know it's real?"

"You can soak it in a solution of one part isopropyl alcohol to one part water and then try to set it on fire. A chemistry professor showed me once. If it's real money, it won't burn."

I put the bills in my pocket. "Thanks, but I'll just take your word for it." We pushed the broken glass to the side of the alley near a wall. Then I helped her with a wrist roll.

"You know, you're not half bad for a—"

"Weirdo?" she asked.

I was going to say teacher, really I was, but as soon as she filled in the blank like that, a picture of the VJs insulting her on the porch came zooming back to me. I felt bad that we had hurt her feelings, and I didn't know what else to say. "It's just that you're different," I told her.

"Not as different as people often assume."

"But you're a genius."

"At math. That doesn't mean I'm good at everything. Besides, you can catch a spinning baton dropping three stories with your eyes closed. Isn't that different?"

"You totally got me there," I admitted.

It made me think. Maybe I didn't have to settle for the short end of the baton. This meeting with Professor Wigglesmith could be a sign of good things to come. If I practiced, I would pass math, win first place at the Twirlcrazy Grand Championship, and maybe, just maybe, Miss Brenda wouldn't sell the Baton Barn after all. Everything was going to be cool. My stupid, rotten luck was all bridge under the water.

I tossed my baton, did a backflip, closed my eyes, and held out my hand, waiting for the baton to return. I would catch it, Professor Wigglesmith would applaud, and life would be good.

I opened my eyes just as the stupid baton shifted its path and landed with a whack on her head.

9 Aphrodite Calls for a Showdown

The best way to avoid a news reporter is to climb up a tree and act like a nut. Don't ask me how I know this. Even if I had done it, I would never admit it. And Bernie, my squirrel friend from Harvard, would not testify against me for all the Tootsie Rolls in town. I will admit I hate being interviewed. Most reporters don't know enough math to understand my work, so they focus on personal details. They think it's funny that my mother's a plumber and make up headlines like PLUMBER'S CHILD HAS GREAT MATH PIPES and UNCLOGGING THE MYSTERY—HOW A PLUMBER'S DAUGHTER DRAINED THE MATH POOL.

Principal DeGuy waved from the back of the classroom. He was visiting again and had brought a guest—a reporter who was doing a feature story on me. The reporter was himself a graduate of Carnegie Middle School, where he was best remembered as the soloist who sang "Hark the Hairy Angels Sing" at a Christmas concert.

The reporter was staring at Roland, who was in the front of the classroom making pistachio ice cream. Roland measured out one cup of milk, two teaspoons of sugar, and one tablespoon of imitation pistachio extract into a small freezer bag. Then he took a larger freezer bag, filled it with four cups of ice, and added 1/4 cup of salt. He placed the small bag inside the big bag, sealed it, and danced like a crazed rock star to shake the concoction.

It was not exactly what I had expected when I announced today would be a "Why Math Matters to Me Day," but I couldn't have been more pleased. After Mindy had demonstrated her baton skills for me in the alley, I realized that math affects my students' everyday lives as much as mine. So I challenged each of them to think about a favorite hobby or interest and do a presentation for the class that showed the mathematics involved (for extra credit, of course). Roland had been my first volunteer.

"Math matters to me because without it I couldn't

make ice cream," he had said when he began. "Cooking is a very mathematical thing. It uses fractions, ratios, weights, volume, temperature, and time. You multiply a recipe when you're in a sharing mood and want to make enough for everyone, and you divide when you're feeling like a pig and want to make just enough for yourself."

When Roland stopped shaking, he opened the bag and squirted a mushy helping of hand-shaken pistachio ice cream into his mouth. Then he grabbed his heart as if to suggest the ice cream was so good it could kill him. "In conclusion, math tastes good."

The bell rang and the students sprang for the door, but the reporter caught me before I could steal away.

"I'm Stanley Butera," he said. "Delighted to meet you, Professor Wigglesmith."

"I hope you enjoyed the class," I replied, inching toward the exit.

Principal DeGuy took me by the arm. "Stan covers all the school activities for us."

"My favorite is the Great Math Showdown," the reporter said. "It's a quiz-type competition for the eighth-grade math classes here at the middle school, sponsored by Right Type Office Supply Store. The winning team gets two hundred dollars. Last year's team used it to buy new calculators and give their classroom a makeover. Mr. Ripple, your honors math teacher, runs the competition."

"How interesting," I said. And I wasn't just being polite. It was the most exciting news I'd heard since I began teaching. New calculators would be a well-deserved reward for all the work my students had been doing, and my classroom could certainly use a makeover. But, more important, if my remedial math class entered the Great Math Showdown and won, it would prove my theory that anyone could be a math wiz.

"You should encourage your students to watch," the reporter added. "It would probably be a thrill for them to see the smart students solving equations."

It made me want to give him a thrill in the nose, the way he said "smart students"—as if my students were stupid. I would speak to Mr. Ripple, but not about getting my students good seats so they could watch the competition. I would talk to him about entering my students in the Great Math Showdown as an official team; the only watching they would do would be to watch the judges hand them the trophy.

The teachers' lounge was located beside the adult restrooms and as far away from the band room as possible.

There were three unwritten rules: don't hang your coat on a more senior teacher's hook; don't compare salaries; and (for reasons that would later become clear) don't allow your pet tarantulas to run loose.

Mr. Ripple took a huge bite out of his baloney sandwich and talked as he chewed. He had tight skin and a pencil-thin mustache that wiggled as he ate. "Only the gifted and academic math classes enter the Great Math Showdown," he said. "There are advanced problems, so there's no way your students could win."

"But no rule prohibits my students from entering, right?"

Mr. Ripple bit off another chunk of sandwich, while the handful of other teachers present listened. "Little lady, you'd be setting them up for failure. Why would you want to embarrass them like that? Remedial math students should focus on remedial math and leave the showdown to the other classes."

I peeled my orange and gave him a sour look. He opened a bag of potato chips and crunched loudly. Once, while I attended Carnegie Middle School, Mr. Ripple briefly had been my math teacher. He didn't seem to like me then, and he didn't seem to like me now. It was not my wish to embarrass my students, but how else could I get the rest of the school to stop treating them like boneheads?

"It's a self-fulfilling prophecy," I mumbled.

"What's that?" asked Mr. Ripple, brushing crumbs off his shirt.

"Nothing."

He bit another chip.

I said, "It's just that, if we expect my students to fail, they will expect themselves to fail. If everyone expects failure, that's the result."

Mrs. Underwood, the district's reading specialist, chimed in. "Really, sweetie, you're not suggesting intelligence is irrelevant? You of all people should realize that some students are born with more upstairs."

"Know what they call my students?" I asked.

Silence.

Finally, Mr. Ripple responded. "Everybody knows. Boneheads."

"Do you know how that makes them feel?" I asked.

"Probably like boneheads."

"That's the problem," I said.

Mr. Ripple crunched another chip.

"Intelligence isn't as much about ability as it is about the time required to learn something," I continued. "Success requires confidence and effort. The students in my class simply aren't used to exploiting their full potential."

"If you say so, sweetie," said Mrs. Underwood.

"Sweetie" and "little lady" were words adults often used to suggest I should shut up, but I would not be deterred. "How can I ask my students to believe in themselves if we don't believe in them? Winning the Great Math Showdown is exactly what my students need to prove they, too, can be math wizzes."

"And losing the competition is exactly what those poor students don't need." Mr. Ripple dropped his baloney sandwich. He wagged his finger at me like he was scolding a puppy. "You're expecting too much. Assuming they can beat the gifted and academic classes."

"I believe," I told him, "that given sufficient instruction and motivation, almost anyone can be a math wiz."

"Maybe," he said. "And maybe frogs can fly."

It was the same thing Principal DeGuy had once said. The other teachers were nodding madly. They were so set in their ways, they weren't even listening. If only they realized how much progress my students had already made. They were doing the harder work and doing it well. But if the rest of the world still treated them like boneheads, they might lose confidence and stop trying. I could never prove my theory if that happened.

I gathered my orange peels and placed them in my brown bag. From the corner of my eye, I caught a movement. Something was scurrying across the floor, something fist-sized and hairy.

"Tarantula!" Mrs. Underwood screamed.

Mr. Green, the biology teacher, dropped on all fours and followed the spider. "Romeo, or Juliet, whichever one you are, I've got you this time."

In the end, things were just as they had been before I went to the lounge. Mr. Green's pet tarantulas (which I later learned were mascots for the Carnegie Spiders wrestling team) remained on the loose, and, to the other teachers, my students remained boneheads. But things were about to change.

10 Mindy Has a Meltdown

I decided to put it to a class vote," Professor Wigglesmith told us the next day. She was wearing another one of her boring gray suits, and it made me think: *If a yawn had a color it would probably be gray.* Anyway, she told us all about the Great Math Showdown and said winning it would prove to everyone we weren't hopeless dolts. A lot of the kids seemed to be buying it, but I happen to be a little more careful about what I put in my shopping cart.

"The competition will require practice, but you'll get extra credit, and that will go a long way toward helping you pass class," she said. "Those who think we should enter the competition?" Adam, Keisha, Eugenia, Salvador, Hunter, LeeAnn, and Roland raised their hands. "That makes seven. Anyone else?" She turned to put the number on the board, writing it low, probably to avoid having to use the dreaded stool.

While her back was turned, Roland held up a paper that said *Vote for the competition or I'll breathe on you.*

Bobby raised his hand. "Me too," he said. "I'll vote for it."

Professor Wigglesmith changed the number to eight. "Those who don't want to compete?" Eight other kids raised their hands. "We can't make a decision with a tie. Who didn't vote?"

"Mindy didn't vote," said Roland.

"Shut up and mind your own business," I said, slumping down in my chair. Getting my math grade up was one thing; wasting my time on some lame math contest was another. There were two good reasons not to do it. First, I had to stay focused on getting ready for the Twirlcrazy Grand Championship, which was coming up and might be my last chance to compete, since the Baton Barn was closing. Second, I might have been stupid, but not stupid enough to believe I was smarter than the smart kids.

"Mindy? What about you? I know you could use the extra credit. If we set the practices later in the evening, you would still have time for your baton."

I leaned back in my seat. "Sorry, I don't think so."

Professor Wigglesmith was wasting her time. I already had a solid C, and between class and after-school tutoring, I spent enough time on math. Nothing could make me give up free time to crunch more numbers.

"Come on," said Adam. "Give us your vote." From the tone in his voice, he was practically begging.

He locked eyes with me, and a tingle crept up my spine. Adam's smile was so sweet I gained two pounds. After all the new lip gloss and cute outfits I had tried, I finally had his attention. "Okay," I said. "As a favor for you, Adam."

Cheers and boos followed, but I kept my gaze on Adam. Call me crazy, but when he mouthed the words "Thank you," I swear my chair lifted six inches off the ground.

"I will advise Mr. Ripple to include us in the Great Math Showdown," Professor Wigglesmith said. "For those who raised their hands, six will be on the class team and the other three will be alternates. After class, we'll meet to set a team practice schedule. The competition is in only nine weeks, so we begin practicing immediately."

"What? You mean we have to practice for nine whole weeks?" asked Roland.

"We must work hard if we want to win," Professor

Wigglesmith said. "Now, who wants to be team captain?"

Timothy raised his hand.

"You have to be on the team to be the captain," said Professor Wigglesmith, smiling.

Adam raised his hand. "I volunteer," he said.

Professor Wigglesmith blushed. *She's got a crush on him,* I thought. *Like every other thirteen-year-old girl.* But the idea of Professor Wigglesmith with Adam was so ridiculous it was hard to take seriously.

We practiced three evenings a week at the Carnegie Diner. So that I could make it on time, Professor Wigglesmith's dad would drive me to my class at the Baton Barn and then drop us both off at the diner afterwards. That was fine by me, since it beat the icicle ears I got when I biked there.

We were usually the first to arrive at the diner, and would take the two tables in the back and push them together. Today, just to shake things up, we ordered for each other. I ordered her cheese fries and a killer burger. She ordered me some stupid salad with gross little chunks of chicken and this runny low-fat dressing. That shook me up, all right!

It had rained earlier in the day and the slippery streets were slowing traffic, so it was taking longer than usual for the rest of the math team to show. I dropped my straw, and when I bent down to pick it up, I noticed Professor Wigglesmith's feet dangling. "You don't even touch the floor when you sit," I observed.

"We're all on the short side in my family. I'm only four feet, six inches," she admitted. "It's a genetic predisposition. My father says we're remotely descended from General Napoleon, although my history professor at Harvard said Napoleon's stature was grossly underestimated."

At five feet, six inches, I was a solid foot taller than Professor Wigglesworth. "Doesn't it bother you to be so short?" I asked.

"Sometimes," she said, pushing bangs out of her eyes. "Like when I want to write high on the board and I have to pull up that awful stool."

She shuddered, and I could almost hear it fart. Half of me wanted to tell her about the hidden whoopee cushion so she could stop embarrassing herself, but the other half didn't want to go to detention for not telling her sooner.

"Does it ever bother you to be so tall?" she asked.

"When I was in elementary school I got called 'Jolly Green Giant' so many times, I banished the color from my wardrobe. I still won't wear green."

"I've worn something pink every day since I was four," she replied.

"Really?" I asked skeptically. I mean, after that day she came to my house in the bright pink pants and pastel pink jacket, I hadn't seen her wear pink once.

"Even at Harvard, when I went to a Mensa meeting, I would wear a black or gray suit, but secretly wear something pink where nobody could see. Are you aware how many shades of pink there are?"

"Three?" I guessed.

"There's amaranth pink, bubblegum pink, carnation pink, cerise pink, cherry blossom, coral pink, dark pink, deep pink, French rose, fuchsia—"

"I get the idea."

"Hot pink, Japanese pink, lavender pink, pink magenta, Persian pink, Pink Panther pink, salmon, shocking pink, tea rose, and thulium pink, just to name a few. Flamingo is my favorite." She lifted the bottom of her black pants and showed me her flamingo pink socks.

"Can I ask a question? I mean, if you like pink so much, why don't you just wear it without worrying about if people can see it?"

"Last time I did that, someone said I looked like a piece of bubblegum stuck in a cotton candy machine." The words I had spoken sounded a lot meaner when she repeated them back to me. She added, "I assumed you were suggesting I not dress that way again."

"Do you always do things just because other people tell you to?" I asked. It was meant as one of those questions that you aren't really supposed to answer, but she paused as if giving it deep thought.

"Usually," she said. "Do you think I should I stop?"

I tried to match the insecure girl sipping root beer with my self-confident math teacher. "Can I ask you a question? Why do you act so different after school?"

"I'm supposed to act like a teacher when I'm in class. I'm not supposed to act like me."

At first, that sounded pretty weird, but then when I thought about it, I realized what she meant. "Like when I'm at a baton competition," I said. "I'm supposed to act like I'm having a great time, even if I have to do a split when I really need to pee, or if I accidentally send a hoop baton sailing into the crowd."

"Sort of like that," she said.

We talked a while about how people expect you to act one way when you feel like acting another, and then I told her about the Baton Barn becoming a Cluck and Shuck, which she agreed was totally wrong. Then to blow some more time, I had her give me her hand so I could read her palm. Not that I was a real palm reader or anything, but since I did a lot of manicures Mom had shown me the location of the lines that were supposed to mean something. She said people would give extra tips if I spotted a long fame or luck line.

"Here's something," I told Professor Wigglesmith. "Look at all the distance between your life line and your love line."

"Is that bad?" she asked.

"I don't know," I answered. "This is usually when I try to make up something nice so I'll get a good tip. Like, if you were a customer, I might say: It means you will soon find a new love to fill the space." Speaking of love . . . In anticipation of Adam's arrival, I got out my cherry-scented lip gloss and slathered it on. I also checked the polish on my nails.

As I spun my fork, Professor Wigglesmith counted out loud the number of spins. She was one strange cookie, that Professor Wigglesmith. Not the kind of person I would normally hang out with, yet we got along just fine, even if I had only joined the team to be with Adam.

"Have you ever wondered," I asked, "what would have happened if you hadn't been so smart? I mean, if you were just regular. You'd be an eighth grader at Carnegie Middle School, just like me. We might have even been friends."

"Aren't we friends now?" she asked.

That took me by surprise. "You're my teacher," I said, setting the fork down. "That would be too weird."

Roland and Salvador stumbled in and found our table. "Did you order yet?" asked Salvador.

Professor Wigglesmith smiled. "I'm having cheese fries and a killer burger."

"Ugh! You've corrupted her," said Roland.

Salvador plopped beside me. "That seat's saved for Adam," I told him.

He pretended to examine the chair. "I don't see his name on it."

Boys! I remembered when we were in third grade and I thought Salvador was cute. He came up to me all sweet and innocent and asked if I wanted gum. I said yes and he pulled a wad out of his mouth and stuck it on my nose. That was the day I crossed him off my "potential boyfriend" list.

I wanted Salvador to move, but if I made too much of a fuss, he would tease me about liking Adam and then Adam would walk in and it would be a disaster. "Whatever," I said.

Practice lasted one and a half hours, and my salad was so awful I had to beg Professor Wigglesmith to trade so I wouldn't starve. That was the bad news. The good news was that doing math together in a group made it bearable, and Professor Wigglesmith said we were making great progress. When practice was over, she rushed off to plan "a surprise." The rest of us scattered. I started to walk home, but heard someone behind me, turned, and saw Adam.

"Hey, Mindy, wait up. Can I walk with you?"

"Sure." Adam lived on the other side of town, so walking me home was totally a good sign.

"Cool, isn't it?"

"I don't know. Except for the puddles, I think it's kind of nice out."

"No. The other cool. I mean, the math team and the competition and all?"

Why did I have to be so stupid? "Oh, yeah, I guess."

"Miss Wigglesmith's not like the other teachers."

"Of course not," I said. "She's thirteen."

"I mean, she doesn't look down on us like some of the other teachers do, and she doesn't assume that we're lazy just because we don't get all the answers right."

When I dreamed of having Adam to myself, this

was not the conversation I had in mind. "So, are you going to the dance?" I asked.

"What dance?"

"You know, *the* dance, the Spring Fling, next month. I totally wanted to go last year, but they have that stupid rule about having to be in eighth grade."

"I hadn't thought about it." He shifted his backpack. "I've been so busy with the Great Math Showdown, it's almost like I've been living in another world. My dad's an engineer, you know."

I shrugged, wondering what that had to do with anything.

"He was really disappointed about my math grade when we had Miss Snipal. Not that he rubbed it in or anything; still, I knew. He tried to help with my homework, but you know how parents are."

"Oh," I said, wondering how to steer the conversation to the dance. This was my big chance to score a date with a total hottie, but Adam wasn't making it easy.

He ran a hand through his prickly blond hair. "You should have seen him when I said we were entering the Great Math Showdown and that I was team captain. I've taken home a lot of trophies for wrestling and basketball, but my parents care more about academics. Winning the Great Math Showdown would really mean something to them."

"I've got about a million twirl trophies," I said.

"Twirl?"

"You know, baton twirling."

."Oh."

"That's how a lot of people react. They think it's just a bunch of girls in sparkly leotards playing with metal sticks. The thing is, nowadays, it's treated more like a real sport. Countries from all over, like Japan, Poland, and South Africa, have teams that compete in the World Championships. Baton is even part of the Junior Olympics. If enough countries participated, it could become an Olympic sport." Then I remembered I was trying to get a date, not to give a baton appreciation lesson. "Plus there's dancing in it, too. Do you like to dance?"

"I don't know," said Adam.

We were at the beauty shop.

"This is where I live, above the shop. My mom is the Tiffany part of Tiffany's House of Beauty and Nails." I pointed to the sign with this week's saying: "Bald Man's Special: Buy One Cut & Blow Dry, Get One Free."

"Oh," said Adam. He hesitated, and my heart raced. *Is he going to kiss me?*

"So, what's she like?" Adam asked.

"My mother, Tiffany?"

"Of course not." Even his laugh was cute. "I know she's tutored you a lot. You probably know her better than any of us."

It hit me like a bare foot in a cold puddle. "Professor Wigglesmith?"

Adam fumbled with his backpack. "Yeah."

If my eyelids had opened any wider, the eyeballs would have popped out and rolled down the street. "Do you like her or something?"

"No," said Adam. "I mean, yes. I mean, not like that. I'm just really glad that she's my teacher."

"Because if you like her, that would be gross, maybe even illegal. I don't think you're allowed to like your teacher, even if she is your age."

"Don't make a major deal out of it," he said. "I just think it's cool that she believes in us. That's all. What's wrong with that?"

"Besides, she's not even pretty."

"She's not?"

I was getting really heated. Why was he going on about Professor Wigglesmith when I was standing there waiting for him to kiss me? "You're completely clueless," I told him.

"Where did that come from?"

"You want to know what I think of Professor Wigglesmith?" I asked. "Here's what I think: she's a total egghead and a complete geek. She thinks she's so smart, running around doing equations like a head with its chicken cut off. But she must be stupid, because only a total idiot would waste her time teaching bonehead math."

"The expression is 'a chicken with its head cut off,'" Adam said. "And that's the difference between her and you; she would never call you stupid."

He turned and walked away. My big mouth had done it again. I wished someone would invent a vacuum cleaner that people could turn on to suck back words that they said in anger but didn't really mean. They could call it the Mindy-Did-It-Again-Vac, since I would be its number-one customer.

"Wait!" I said. "I can explain. Come back!"

He kept walking.

"Okay." I yelled. "I've got to go in now. See you tomorrow."

I reached for the doorknob while keeping my gaze on him. I wanted to see if he would steal a glance back to make sure I was okay, but he didn't.

11 Aphrodite Takes Aim
at the Problem

Just because a person is a rocket scientist, that doesn't mean he knows how to sew a button on his underwear. Yet there are people who think geniuses always know what they're doing. Principal DeGuy was like that with me. I could wear a kangaroo on my head and he'd assume the extra pocket made it a wise fashion choice. No matter what my suggestion, he always gave me thumbs up.

"Did I hear right?" Miss Snipal asked. "You're taking your math class on a field trip to a pool hall?"

I nodded. I was working on mathematical theory for the Navier-Stokes problems in my diary over lunch. But there were so many teachers in the lounge it was hard to concentrate.

"Letting those students go on a field trip is a big mistake," said Mr. Green.

"You'd better bring plenty of chaperones," added Mrs. Underwood. "And make sure the school's liability insurance will cover it, too."

"Have you ever been to a pool hall?" asked Mr. Ripple from his stuffed chair near the door. "Do you know what kind of people frequent pool halls?"

As usual, he'd brought potato chips and was making a crunchy mess. Romeo and Juliet, the tarantulas, hadn't been caught, and I couldn't help imagining that they were living off Mr. Ripple's droppings.

"A field trip should relate to what students are learning," said Mrs. Underwood. "Whatever do you hope to accomplish at a pool hall?"

I closed my diary. "The game of pocket billiards," I said, "commonly called pool, can teach about angles, because whether an angle is ninety-five degrees or eighty-five degrees will make the difference between the ball going into the pocket or not."

"I suppose I should take my biology class to a health spa to show the effects of a whole-body massage on the circulatory system," said Mr. Green.

"I'm sure they'd enjoy that," I replied.

"Little lady, a pool hall is not an appropriate place for a field trip," Mr. Ripple said. "You'll be explaining that decision to angry parents for weeks."

I wanted to tell him he was wrong, but it wouldn't matter. I had met a lot of people like Mr. Ripple—closed-minded to new ways of doing things. I tossed my apple core in my lunch bag. As I passed by Mr. Ripple, I tried to formulate a pithy comeback. I stared him straight in the eye. He looked a bit odd with his toupee crooked. Then I realized he wasn't wearing a toupee. "Tarantula!" I screamed.

The next day, I told the class, "I have good new and bad news. The good news is that the testing we did last class showed a thirty-two percent increase in scores." The class erupted. I held out my hands for silence. "The bad news," I said teasingly, "is that I will not be able to teach class on Friday."

"What gives?" asked Roland.

Mindy shot up in her seat. "You're not leaving us?"

"Of course not," I said. "You won't be here, either. I've arranged for you to be excused from your Friday classes because we're going on a field trip!"

The celebration resumed.

"We are about to start a geometry subsection," I said. "So I thought you might like to see a practical application of angles."

"We're going to a geometry museum?" Roland guessed.

"No," I said. "We're going to the Shoot-M-Up pool hall on East Third Street." They were cheering and clapping so loudly, it felt like the room would spin.

On Friday, a bus picked us up at the school's back entrance. I sat in the front so I could count students getting on and off. Mindy said she got "bus sick" and was less likely to throw up if she sat up front, too, and I was happy to offer her the seat next to me.

The Shoot-M-Up pool hall was across the railroad tracks on the other side of town. It was usually closed during the day, pool being more of an evening recreation. However, I had made arrangements with the manager, Mr. Finch.

He was a short, chubby man with a bald head and a handlebar mustache. Colorful tattoos peeked out of the ends of his shirtsleeves, and he wore cowboy boots with pointed tips. Mr. Finch had a couple of his regular customers come by to help us with the basics. Contrary to the teachers' warnings, Mr. Finch was well-mannered and genuinely eager to help. He wouldn't even accept the small stipend from the school's field trip fund.

"I consider it my civic duty," Mr. Finch said. "Just because you run a pool hall, or your kid threw a firecracker down a school toilet and caused a flood back when he was twelve, doesn't mean you're not as good a citizen as the rest."

The students had gabbed madly on the bus to the pool hall. But when they filed inside, they fell quiet, looking around as if they were really in a geometry museum.

"First off, you each get one of these," said Mr. Finch as pool sticks were passed. The students made mock pool shots in the air. Mr. Finch grabbed Mindy's stick and turned it around. "Works better if you hit the ball with the thin end of the stick," he said.

Nine pool tables were spread apart in three rows of three. Above each table was a fluorescent light in a stained-glass fixture. We would play 8-ball. Mr. Finch explained the game as Angel, a burly man in a purple suit jacket, and Bruno, a dark-skinned man with a huge Afro, demonstrated. On each table, fifteen balls were herded together in a plastic triangle. Eight were solid and seven striped. One player had to knock the solid-color balls in the pockets and the other player had to knock in the striped balls. The black 8-ball would go in last.

I put two students each at the pool tables; Mr.Finch joined them to make it even. The instructors—Angel, Bruno, Snake, Freddy, and Princess—demonstrated how to chalk the sticks and "break" the balls to start the game. During the demonstration, I grabbed a stick and sunk bank shots.

"I never would have figured you for the pool hall type," Roland said.

"We all have secrets," I replied.

Actually, I had never been to a pool hall. I had picked up the game while at Harvard. When I felt homesick, I would go to the recreation room at Dr. Goode's house and play with Hershey Bear. Calculating the correct angles, I could usually sink every ball in order.

"Professor Wigglesmith!" yelled LeeAnn. "I got a hole in one!"

"They're all holes in one in this game," I said. "What was your angle?"

"Forty-five degrees. But I wasn't even aiming for the hole it went in."

I had explained the rules on the bus ride. Before you take a shot, I said, you must decide what the best angle would be to hit the white cue ball to get the other ball in the pocket, and write down the degree of the angle. I explained how to use the specially designed protractors I'd brought to determine the angles.

"Professor Wigglesmith," called Salvador. "Isn't there a limit? Eugenia got two balls in a row and now she wants to take another turn."

"Sorry," said Eugenia. "I didn't know I would be good at this. I'm awful at sports."

"It's all right. As long as you get the ball in the pocket, you may take as many shots as you'd like."

I wandered from table to table, giving encouragement. After a while, I was having so much fun, I almost forgot I was the teacher and the other thirteen-year-olds were my students. The volunteers from the pool hall were fascinated by the protractors.

"Mind if I try?" asked Snake, a skinny man with two gold teeth.

"Go ahead," said Keisha, handing him a protractor.

Snake measured and sunk the ball. "I gotta get me one of these things," he said.

It was 11:30 when a student asked about eating, and I realized that we had left our packed lunches on the bus.

"It won't be back for hours," said Roland. "We're gonna starve to death."

I thought about calling the school to see if someone could bring them over, but when I pictured Mr. Ripple hearing about my mistake, it made me cringe. I gathered my nerve. "Mr. Finch, I wonder if you could open your snack bar?"

"No problem," he said. "Lunch is on the house."

The snack bar special was nacho chips with cheese, chili, and peppers. I had a salad made from the lettuce used for the cheeseburgers.

"This is my idea of a field trip," said Roland as he loaded peppers on his nachos. He and the other boys spun on the bar stools.

For dessert, Mr. Finch set the candy machine to dispense selections without money. The students lined up and worked it like an arcade slot machine. By afternoon, the class was not only good with pool sticks and protractors, but seemed to have made new friends. Snake showed Mindy how he could sink a shot using the folding baton she brought along, and Mindy showed Snake how he could twirl his pool stick like it was a baton.

Mr. Finch seemed sad to see us go.

"Take a souvenir," he said, passing out tiny cubes of blue chalk. "Tell your friends and parents we run a friendly place here."

"Can I see your tattoos?" LeeAnn asked. Mr. Finch raised his shirtsleeve to reveal a boat on his biceps. As he flexed his muscle, the boat traveled on a painted wave.

"Too cool," said Hunter.

"Check out this one," Mr. Finch said. He bent forward, showing off the four-leaf clover tattooed on the center of his bald head. "If you touch it, it'll bring you good luck."

On their way out, each student patted the top of his head. I was the last to go. "That was thoroughly enjoyable and educational," I told Mr. Finch. I reached into my book bag. "Here are twenty thank-you tickets for you and your helpers."

"You don't have to give us nothing," Mr. Finch protested.

"Please," I said. "They're for the Great Math Showdown. We're the underdogs, and your support would mean a lot to us. Come if you can."

Mr. Finch took the tickets. "Maybe we will." He tilted his head forward. "Hey, you want to rub my tattoo?"

I blushed.

"Go ahead," said Mr. Finch. "For luck, for your math contest. They're a smart bunch of kids, but everybody can do with a bit o' luck, right?"

I pictured Mr. Ripple again, this time crunching

his potato chips as my team stood for the competition. In my imagination, the students from his gifted math class were equally smug and also crunching chips.

I reached for Mr. Finch's tattoo. "One can never have too much luck."

12 Mindy Takes Aphrodite Shopping

Veronica Breech had been my friend since second grade, but no matter what I did, she totally went out of her way to outdo me. Her parents divorced when she was a baby, and her mom and dad thought they could prove they loved her by giving her a stack of credit cards. So if I got a cell phone, Veronica got an iPhone. If I went to the arcade, Veronica got a trip to Disney World. Once I thought about jumping in the creek, just to see if she would jump in the river.

"Why do you hang out with that girl?" Mom asked. "If she's a friend, I'm a moose."

My mom was not a moose. The sad fact was that I hung out with Veronica because she was popular, and hanging out with popular people made me more popular.

Anyway, a few weeks after the pool hall trip, Veronica was waiting outside math class for me. I had bought these awesome sunglasses last time we went shopping—white Ray-Bans marked down to almost nothing on clearance because they had a scratch you could really barely see—and to one-up me, Veronica ordered these cool new "Color of the Week" contacts. The day she was waiting outside of math class for me, her eyes were violet to match her new blouse.

"Are you going to the spring dance?" Veronica asked.

"Have I ever missed a chance to wear three-inch heels?" I replied.

"Details! How many boys have asked you, and who's Mr. Lucky?"

"Three have asked, but I'm not sure who to pick."

"Me neither," said Veronica. "Only, I got asked by four guys. Sometimes I wish I wasn't so popular—just kidding."

At Carnegie Middle School, the Spring Fling was the big event of the year. I had waited an entire week for Adam to ask me, dressing especially amazing each day and even curling my hair. No matter what I did, he wasn't interested. Yesterday, I asked him if he wanted to walk me home again, but he said he had to get to basketball practice. The boys who asked me to the dance were okay, but Adam was the most sought-after boy in the eighth grade, and the girl on his arm would have the power to turn all the other girls at the dance instantly green. At least he hadn't asked Veronica. That would have been a fate worse than Adamlessness.

"I totally know what you mean," I told her. "I still have to go shopping. It's not gonna be easy to find the perfect dress to complement my ringlets updo. That's how Mom's doing my hair."

"Can she do mine?" Veronica asked.

"I guess. But you better get an appointment, because she always fills up when there's a dance."

"We should get a group together and all go to your mom's beauty salon and get our hair and nails done before the dance."

"Cool," I said. "I'll set it up."

Professor Wigglesmith came to the door. "Time for class."

"What about you?" I asked her. "Are you going?"

"Going where?"

"To the dance—you know, the Spring Fling."

"I don't suppose I'm allowed," said Professor Wigglesmith, brushing her bangs away from her eyes. "I believe it's for students."

"Why don't you go as a chaperone?" I suggested.

"I have no experience. Besides, I wouldn't know what to wear."

"Oh, come on," I said. "The dances here are awesome. You should totally go."

Professor Wigglesmith blushed and turned back into her classroom. Then I noticed Veronica's expression—a cross between shock and horror.

"Why would you encourage *her* to go to the dance?" asked Veronica.

From the look in her eyes, I realized my mistake. Inviting a teacher to an after-school event was way uncool. Between her coming to my house for tutoring and us goofing around together at the Carnegie Diner waiting for the rest of the math team to show, I had spent so much time with Professor Wigglesmith that sometimes I forgot we weren't supposed to be friends. I had to think of something fast. "How else am I gonna get my math grade up? Tell me you don't kiss up to teachers for extra points."

"That's all it is? Because Jordeen told me her cousin Sarah saw you and Professor Wigglesmith hanging out together at the Carnegie Diner."

"It's that stupid math team," I said.

"So she's not, like, your friend?"

"Think about it," I said. "Aphrodite Wigglesmith, biggest geek ever, friends with me?" I put my outstretched thumb and index finger against my forehead in the form of an "L," the universal sign for loser. "I think not."

Veronica headed off to class looking satisfied, and I went into math class and took my seat. It was another one of those "Why Math Matters to Me" days, and Eugenia was passing out balls of black yarn and giant needles.

"Math matters to me because knitting is my favorite thing to do, and without math I couldn't knit a thing," Eugenia said. "Understanding patterns, maintaining symmetry, and calculating stitch ratios are all math concepts used in the textile arts." Then she showed everyone how to use math to "cast on" the yarn with knitting needles.

Timothy raised his hand. "What do you call a clever sweater maker?" he asked. "A knit-wit. Get it?"

Half the class groaned.

While I looped the yarn on my needle, I replayed in my mind what had just happened in the hallway when I accidentally invited Professor Wigglesmith to come to the school dance. It was strange. Even though she was my teacher, there were a lot of reasons I liked hanging out with her. She didn't treat me like I was stupid all the time like my other "friends" did. Plus, when I was with girls like Veronica, Jordeen, and Summer, they always wanted to compete over who had the smoothest skin, or shiniest hair, or whitest teeth. With Professor Wigglesmith, I didn't have to compete. I could just be myself. Still, I had to be careful, because she was a certified geek and I was popular. Hanging out with Professor Wigglesmith could ruin my reputation.

The next week, when Professor Wigglesmith asked if I would go with her to pick out a dress for the dance, I was careful to meet her at the South Hills Village Mall. We were less likely to be spotted there because it was farther from town. Right away, I knew I'd made the right decision. Professor Wigglesmith stared in clueless awe at everything from the food court to the mechanical dogs barking by the toy store.

"You're acting like you've never been in a mall before," I said. "Doesn't your mom take you shopping?"

Professor Wigglesmith stopped in front of a bank of gum machines. "While I was at Harvard I was always too busy with my schoolwork to go shopping, so I got in the habit of buying my clothes from a mail-order catalog. Why would anyone choose to eat something called a bloody eyeball?"

"It's gum," I said. "It's got a cherry liquid center, so it squirts when you bite into it. Totally gross."

While she gawked at the gumball machine, I backed up and practiced figure eights. I brought my baton most everywhere I went so I could get in as much practice as possible before the Twirlcrazy Grand Championship. Miss Brenda had decided I was ready to try a two-baton routine, and had taught me some off-the-chart, totally trophy-worthy tricks. I meant to perfect them. I couldn't stop the Baton Barn from closing, but I could take home first place at my last competition.

"Follow me," I told Professor Wigglesmith, taking her in the direction of Hip Dip, a teen chain that follows the trends. "I know a store you'll love."

We went over to the dress section, where all the dresses were arranged by color. Professor Wigglesmith went straight for the plain, dark dresses. "Something appropriate for a chaperone," she said. But the whole time she was eyeing a section of pink dresses.

I convinced her that she should let me pick some dresses for her to try on since, between the two of us, I was the fashion expert. "Trust me," I said. "I know a lot about making smart clothes choices, because on my crummy allowance I can't afford to buy something that just sits in the closet." I loaded up her arms with a rainbow of dresses, then grabbed a half-dozen of the hottest new styles for myself.

In the dressing room, I slipped on a sunflower yellow silky dress in a size five. The decorative zipper running down the front took forever to zip up, but it was worth it. The color, style, fabric—it all worked.

The fitting room attendant checked out my profile in the three-sided mirror. "You look fabulous," she said.

"I do." *Ignore me now, Adam,* I thought as I smoothed the fabric.

"You've got to see this one," I yelled to Professor Wigglesmith through her dressing room door. "What's taking you so long?" When she didn't answer, I tapped on her door. When it flew open, there she was in a strapless lilac dress, with a T-shirt showing underneath. "What a mess," I laughed. "You can't try on a dress with your T-shirt on."

"But it's half naked up top," she said.

"And those thin straps you have your arms in are actually the loops that are used to hold the dress on the hanger. You need to get your arms out of them and tuck them inside the dress."

"But without the straps, how will I hold it up?"

I nudged her back into the dressing room. "Grandma Lucy always says if you can get a dress tight enough, nature will hold it up for you." But even without the T-shirt, the dress was a mess. She could have used the top for a sock drawer and still not have filled it up. "Turn for me." Professor Wigglesmith clomped around in a circle, holding up the top of the dress to keep it from slipping. "Try the one with the tan halter neck," I suggested. But her shoulders were too narrow to pull that look off, and the halter dress had a strange belt thing that we didn't know what to do with.

The next dress was sky blue on top, ocean blue on bottom, and at least a foot longer than she was; there with so much extra fabric she was drowning in it. The long-sleeved gray one with the mock turtleneck that she tried on next made her look like she was going to a funeral. That was followed by a dress that was the same shade as the Pink Panther cartoon character. As soon as I saw her in it, I started singing the punch line from the lame joke Timothy once told me about the Pink Panther stepping on a bug: *dead-ant, dead-ant . . . dead-ant, dead-ant, dead-ant.*

I went out and got some more dresses for her to try on. Professor Wigglesmith pushed her bangs away from her eyes and sighed. "Maybe this was a bad idea," she said.

I got a bobby pin out of my purse and pushed her

bangs out of her eyes with it. Then I told her to try the next dress on wearing the cool three-inch sandals I'd found in the shoe department.

Meanwhile, I was having the opposite problem. Each of the dresses I had tried on fit perfectly and looked great, even the pink one that Professor Wigglesmith had picked for me to try on. So I chose the way I always had to on my stupid budget, checking price tags and keeping the one that cost the least. It was the sunflower yellow silky dress that I had tried on first. I held the dress against me and smiled. "Don't let it bother you," I yelled over the dressing room wall to Professor Wigglesmith. "Lots of girls have trouble finding clothes."

When I came out of my dressing room, I heard the clerk say, "Wow. That dress was made for you." But she stared right past me. I turned and saw Professor Wigglesmith in a sleek black dress with pastel pink trim that I had picked for her. It had a wide square neck, short sleeves that fell just off the shoulders, and a huge pink bow in the back with long ribbons. The black fabric complemented her pale skin by making it look creamy soft, the pink trim gave it just the right contrast, and the shoes gave the dress the exact height it needed for the ribbons to brush the floor.

"Do you like it?" Professor Wigglesmith asked me.

I was startled at how good she looked. "I guess it's okay," I said.

"It's more than okay," said the attendant. "Honey, I have seen dozens of girls try that dress on, and none made it look that good."

Professor Wigglesmith spun and smiled. "Really?" she asked.

I looked over at the reject rack where I had just hung the same dress. *That's so wrong,* I thought. *I could see getting one-upped in the dressing room by Veronica or Summer or even Jordeen, but Professor Wigglesmith? Wasn't it enough that she was so much smarter than me?*

"Should I buy it?" she asked.

"Whatever," I said. "I'm going to look in the shoe section."

After a dozen pairs, I forgot I was mad at Professor Wigglesmith. The rest of the time we looked for jewelry for her and a new athletic bag that I could use for the Twirlcrazy Grand Championship.

"I've been working on a new two-baton routine," I said. "Miss Brenda says with my flow and glow I have a real shot at first place."

"Your what and who?"

"Flow and glow. It means, you know, my good

rhythm and winning smile. Usually I just try my best and don't worry about where I place, but with the Baton Barn closing and this being my last chance I really want to win."

"How about this one?" asked Professor Wigglesmith, holding up a plum purple bag.

I slid my baton into the long compartment at the bottom; it was a perfect fit. A huge brand name was written across the bag. "This would be great," I said, "if it didn't cost a fortune."

"Let me buy it for you," she offered, "as a good luck present."

"Can I ask a question? I mean, why would you do that?"

"Because we're friends," she said.

I wanted to be straight with her and explain that we weren't officially friends. I wanted to tell her how social standing works in middle school and how guilt by association keeps popular girls like me from openly being close with nerdy girls like her. But the truth was, I wanted the bag more. "Are you sure you wouldn't mind? I could pay you back, Professor Wigglesmith."

"I'll tell you how you could pay me back." She scooped it up and took it to the cashier. "When we're not in school, you can stop calling me Professor Wigglesmith. Call me Aphrodite, or, better yet, by the nickname Hermy uses—Dytee."

I thought that was pretty cool. Professor Wigglesmith—I mean Dytee—acted like she actually cared. I couldn't remember any of my so-called friends ever offering to buy me anything. My school friends never even came to my competitions. They pretended they had other things to do, and I pretended not to care. Sometimes it felt like they actually wanted me to fail so it would make them look better. But Dytee wasn't like that. She had my back. Even though we couldn't be real friends because of my reputation, there was no harm in us being secret after-school-only friends.

"Thanks," I said.

We were supposed to meet her mom at the star court at 9:00 p.m. It was an open area showing off the mall's soaring ceiling. We were a little early, so I practiced my fujimi rolls, using my elbows to roll the baton from front to back.

"Look. There's one of those photo booths," Dytee said, pointing to a Picture Perfect Photo Booth.

"Don't tell me you've never seen a photo booth?"

"Of course I've *seen* one. I've just never actually gone inside one."

"Come on," I said, pulling my last three dollars from

my jeans. "I'll show you how it works. My treat." We ducked into the booth and squeezed next to each other in the hard seat. "Do this," I said, putting my arms over my head and forming my fingers into a halo. She got her arms halfway up when the flash went off. We both burst out laughing, and the camera caught it all.

As we waited for the photos to come out of the machine, I handed Dytee my baton to hold. She tried to do the fujimi roll, which was totally out of her league, and kept dropping the baton and chasing it around. The strip of photos was peeking out of the slot and I was careful to hold it on the edges so it wouldn't smudge. That's when I noticed Dytee looking up at the ceiling above the star court, then at the baton she was holding.

She spread her legs out for balance, just like she had when she broke the window in the alley outside of my mom's beauty shop. Then she lowered the baton and flung it in the air. It flew at the speed of the sound of my horrified scream, veered sideways, struck a beam, and shot through the front window of the Hip Dip clothing store.

Crash!

"I'm afraid I failed to take that trajectory into account in my equation," said Dytee. She slipped her hand in her pocket, pulled out her wad of Ben Franklins, and rushed toward the store.

A middle-aged woman in a flowered dress standing nearby had witnessed it all. "What kind of an idiot brings a baton to a mall?" she asked.

"People who live in glass stones shouldn't throw houses," I reminded the woman, and went to help Dytee.

13   Aphrodite Dresses Up

In many ways, people are like spiders. Not just because they both have hairy legs and can act creepy. Spiders are creatures of habit, but every now and then, one of them surprises you. Take Romeo and Juliet, for example. After we found Romeo sitting on Mr. Ripple's head, Mr. Green caught him and took him back to his tank in the biology room. I figured Juliet would sense danger and stay hidden. Instead, she played dead in the middle of the room, as if she wanted to be caught so she could be returned to the tank next to Romeo's. That was so unexpected.

Just like, when I approached Mindy in the hallway at school, I wasn't expecting her to ask me if I was going to the Spring Fling, and I certainly wasn't expecting her to agree to go dress shopping at the mall with me. I'd never had a friend my own age before. It was weird—good weird, but weird.

The teachers' lounge had become more relaxing (although less interesting) since the spiders had been caught. I unwrapped my tuna salad sandwich and was about to take a bite when the phone let out a shrill ring.

"It's for you," Mr. Ripple said. "Probably another complaint about your field trip."

Already, I had gotten three calls from parents who questioned why I took their children to a pool hall and demanded that I secure signed field-trip forms in the future. I braced myself to defend the field trip again.

"This is Jeffrey Paul Phillips, local-interest reporter for the *Pittsburgh Post-Gazette* newspaper. I read the article that was printed a few weeks back about you in the *Carnegie Signal Item*."

I recalled my encounter with the *Signal Item* reporter, Stanley Butera. His article about me had focused on my E + C = MW teaching method for remedial students.

"I heard about what's been going on at Carnegie Middle School, and our readers are interested to know more."

I sighed, expecting to be ridiculed in print for taking my students to the pool hall. "I realize my teaching methods may be unusual, but you don't give an antacid to a patient in cardiac arrest."

"Great quote," said the reporter. "I want to hear more about your new teaching method. But first, tell me, what was your reaction when you learned that there had been a forty-eight percent increase in math aptitude test scores among students in your classroom?"

"When did I learn what?" I asked.

"No need to be coy, Professor Wigglesmith. I'm talking about test scores that were released by the Department of Education this morning. Your class has achieved the single-highest increase among students in the state. How does that make you feel?"

My stunned silence answered his question. I knew my students were improving, but even I was dumbfounded by how much. Suddenly, Principal DeGuy appeared. "Aphrodite, you have a call on the line in my office. It's Channel Four news." He took the phone from me. "She'll have to call you back."

"Dytee!" Hermy screamed when my family watched the news that evening.

"Yes, your sister is on television," said Mother.

"Pretty," said Hermy. "Dytee pretty."

"Thank you," I said. Mindy had encouraged me to wear a soft pink blouse under my gray suit jacket for the interview. Mindy's mom had lent me a pair of sparkly clip-on earrings to match. They had tiny hair dryers on them and the phone number for her beauty salon.

"It takes one to know one. Or at least to know how to teach one," said the television voice-over. "This thirteen-year-old has what it takes. Since wiz kid and Harvard graduate Professor Aphrodite Wigglesmith took over the eighth-grade remedial math class at Carnegie Middle School, aptitude scores have soared nearly fifty percent. That's the highest increase in the state."

"They're exceptionally hardworking students," my television self said. "They deserve all the credit."

The camera cut to a classroom of excited students. Roland and LeeAnn pushed to be in the center of the shot.

"But her students say it's their gifted young teacher, Professor Wigglesmith, and her new teaching method that deserve the praise."

A head shot of Adam appeared with a caption: "Adam Boyce, Captain of Mathematics Team."

"Professor Wigglesmith really cares about us and she doesn't treat us like we're stupid," said Adam.

"Having someone believe in you makes you believe in yourself."

"In other news . . ."

Mother snapped off the television. Father rushed through the kitchen door, carrying a gallon of milk. "Did I miss it?"

"Yes," said Mother. "But we got it on videotape."

"I'd have made it," Father said, "but everyone at the supermarket wanted to pass on their congratulations."

"Our Aphrodite is a big star," said Mother.

Hermy pulled his thumb out of his mouth and pointed to the television. "Dytee?" he asked.

"It'll blow over in a week," I said. "Celebrity doesn't last."

The phone rang. I cringed, hoping I would not have to talk about myself anymore.

"It's Mindy," Mother said.

I pounced on the phone. "Did you see it?"

"Of course. Everyone saw it," said Mindy. "I was on TV. You could see me waving in the lower right part of the screen. It was beyond awesome."

I smiled. "My mother recorded it. Do you want to come over tomorrow after math practice and watch?" Silence. "Mindy, are you there?"

"I can't. I've got an extra baton class."

"We can give you a ride."

More silence.

"No," said Mindy. "I'd rather bike. Look, I've got to go."

The line went dead.

14 Mindy Fesses Up

The only reason I lied to Dytee was because telling her I was going shopping with the VJs might have hurt her feelings, and what she didn't know wouldn't. I figured if I saw a better dress than the one I had already bought during my secret shopping trip with Dytee, I could take the first back. As it turned out, I did find a better dress, one that looked so good on me it made the other girls turn "Jolly Green Giant" green. It was perfect.

The day of the dance, eighth-grade girls swarmed Tiffany's House of Beauty & Nails like it was a honeycomb. I wore my new short baby blue dress dotted with reflective sequins. I had dangly silver earrings and a small heart necklace with a matching bracelet. Oodles of ringlets spilled out from my updo and ran down my shoulders.

"You look like you stepped out of here," said my mom, holding a fashion magazine.

The other girls shook their heads jealously, and I played along. "Don't hate me because I'm beautiful."

"Too late," said Summer.

I rubbed a smudge of lipstick off my teeth. "Wait until you see Professor Wigglesmith."

"She showed you her dress?" asked Veronica. The girls looked at me like I was a funeral director at an amusement park.

"Maybe she mentioned it."

The front door shot open and Dytee burst through. The girls turned and snickered, and I couldn't blame them. She was a mess. The beautiful dress I had helped her pick was half covered with an ugly brown shawl. She hadn't put on any of the makeup I had lent her, and she had her hair pulled back in the kind of pony-tail you wear for gym class. I would say that her shoes looked like thrift shop specials, but I wouldn't want to insult the thrift shop.

"OMG!" I said, leading Dytee to a chair. "You look like a baked potato wearing that thing." She took the shawl off, and I dropped it on the counter.

Dytee sat and clutched at her bare shoulders. "I'm afraid I'm a little out of my comfort zone."

"Now you know how Mindy feels in bonehead math," said Veronica. Then she and Jordeen laughed as if their "joke" was actually funny. I ignored them.

"A rubber band for your hair?" I asked Dytee.

"I'm in charge of the punch table," she replied. "I need to be hygienic."

"Hygienic is not the look we're going for." I worked the rubber band free and let Dytee's limp black hair fall just below her shoulders. "That's better," I said. "Now the real work begins."

I pumped the foot control and raised the chair. "Mom!" I yelled. "She's here."

Mom came rushing over. "I'm so excited," she gushed, as if she was about to open a Christmas present. She pulled a plastic covering from a drawer, shook it, and tossed it over Dytee, covering her from the neck down. "I've wanted to get my scissors on that mop since the moment I met you. What's your pleasure? A chic super-straight style? Romantic curls? Just name it."

"Something easy to maintain," said Dytee. "Normally, I don't have much time for things like fancy hairstyles. As a rule, I cut my own hair and keep it simple."

Mom pulled at the ends of her uneven bangs. "Who'd have guessed?" she said. "But keeping it simple is not for Spring Flings. Leave it to me. We're going to make a new girl of you." She spun Dytee around in the chair.

"And Mindy," Mom said, turning to me, "we need to do something about those shoes. Get her that pair you wore to Grandma Lucy's party last year."

By the time I returned, Dytee's face was bright red.

"Maybe she got confused and threw out the shoes and wore the shoe box," said Veronica, holding up one of Dytee's boxy loafers.

"I'll have none of that attitude in my shop," Mom scolded.

Veronica smirked. "Now this," she said, slipping off a hip platform slingback, "is the perfect shoe." She waved it in front of Dytee.

"Yes, quite perfect for you," said Dytee. "A fat heel."

Veronica's mouth dropped, and I burst into laughter.

"I think you've been dissed," said Summer. She gave Dytee a high five.

Jordeen tried to hide a smile, and Veronica stomped over to the magazines and pretended not to care. My mom stared at Dytee.

"I've noticed that insult humor is used by girls my age to bond," Dytee told her. "I hope it wasn't too over the top?"

"You go, girl," Mom said.

Forty minutes later, we were done. Mom had given her the full works, hairstyling, makeup, and manicure. She led Dytee to a full-length mirror.

"Wait until you see," said Summer. "You won't believe the difference."

We stared at her reflection together. Her hair was layered and pinned up in an elaborate bun with two soft strands that spilled down like the cascading ribbon on the back of her dress. Her cheeks were pink, and glittery eye shadow accentuated her eyelids. Her lips and nails were done in a color called Drop Dead Red, and on the tip of each nail was a tiny heart in the exact shade of pastel pink as the trim on her sleek black dress.

"You're beautiful," I said.

"Really?" Dytee asked.

"Not as beautiful as me, of course. But you clean up well."

Mom looked like she might cry. "You're all so grown-up and gorgeous. Now give me hugs, everyone, and let's get you out of here."

"Pictures!" yelled Veronica. "Who has the camera?" The girls vamped as Mom played photographer with their cell phones.

"Now a serious one," said Mom. The girls formed a line in front of the washbasin. Dytee stood on the end next to me. I slipped one arm around Veronica's shoulder and the other around Dytee's. "Say cheese, Louise!"

After pictures, Mom told us to wait out front while she pulled her old Chevy Nova around. It was a real clunker that sometimes needed a push start, so I gave her time to get the car in place, and then we headed out to wait under the sign saying: "If the boss gives you the ax, cheer up with a bikini wax."

But when we stepped outside, there was a stretch limousine in front of the shop. The limousine was white with a pink interior, which we could see through the door that the driver held open.

As he tipped his hat, the chauffeur said, "Ladies."

"Where in blue blazes did that come from?" Mom shouted from the open window of her car.

She looked at me.

I looked at Summer,

Who looked at Veronica,

Who looked at Jordeen,

Who looked at Dytee, who said: "I wasn't sure how many of us there would be, so I requested their biggest car. I hope it's all right."

Almost in unison, we darted for the door, screaming and giggling.

"My instructions," said the driver as we piled in, "are to drive you to the Carnegie Middle School dance and wait."

It was the most awesome thing that had ever happened to me, even including the beginning part of the walk home with Adam. On the ride over, I pretended that Adam had sent the limo and was waiting at the other end for me. I felt so good I might have burst my blue-sequined seams. We pulled in front of the Carnegie Middle School, and everyone strained to see who the limo was carrying.

"Wait," said Veronica. "Let's keep 'em guessing a while."

We watched a crowd gather.

"I can't stand it anymore!" Summer screamed, and she lunged for the door.

The chauffeur hopped out. He took each of our hands and escorted us to the front of the school like we were royalty. Dytee was the last to be walked over to our group. She looked so happy that it made me smile.

Inside, the gymnasium/auditorium was decorated with silver streamers and crepe-paper flowers. On the stage, a real DJ was spinning records, and a bunch of kids were already on the floor. A huge disco ball hung from the ceiling and shot tiny sparkles over everybody, just like you see in the movies.

"This one goes out to Bob from Cynthia," said the DJ as he switched from hip-hop to an old slow song by some guy named Frank. It was "I've Got a Crush on You." The lights dimmed and my heart soared. There was Adam, standing under the scoreboard, wearing black dress pants, a light blue dress shirt, and a silver necktie. He matched my outfit so perfectly it was as if we had planned it.

The girls and I had agreed to meet our dates at the dance, since we didn't think there would be room in Mom's car for everyone. After a few minutes, my date, Timothy, found me and asked if I wanted punch. I said yes, and he hit me on the arm, which was pretty lame, but I totally should have seen it coming. Then I told Timothy I really was thirsty and sent him off to get me punch, even though I only said it to get rid of him so I could stare at Adam. Ten minutes passed with no girl taking his arm. If only Adam asked me to dance.

15   Aphrodite Makes Them Gush

Put sitting at home with your diary and teddy bear on one side. Put a school dance on the other. Then, if you have to choose between them, take the dance. Charles Darwin once said, "A mathematician is a blind man in a dark room looking for a black cat which isn't there." In contrast, I was about to discover, a middle school dancer was like a wiggly person in a sparkly room drinking bubbly punch.

As soon as we arrived at the dance, the girls went off to gossip about who would dance with whom. I stared openmouthed as dots of light from the disco ball swept across my face. They were so delicious I could taste them. Miss Snipal waved me over to the refreshment table.

"What have you done to yourself?" she asked. "I almost didn't recognize you."

Mrs. Underwood checked me out from head to toe. "You look radiant," she said.

"Thank you. See how the pink is just in the trim? The black actually brings emphasis to it. In fashion, you can use one color to complement another," I said, wanting to share Mindy's good advice.

"I'm sure you'll be the loveliest refreshment server at the dance," said Mrs. Underwood. She showed me to the punch bowl. "You pour one part Hawaiian Punch, one part orange juice, and one part ginger ale. Don't let the students take more than two cups at a time, and wait until the level gets below this point before you mix a new batch."

She lifted the tablecloth so I could see the supplies.

"What are the other things?" I asked.

She pointed to an array of industrial-sized glass jars. "This is Hershey's chocolate syrup, for the sundaes, but we only break out the ice cream toward the end of the dance. There's some Tabasco sauce, too, and salsa for the nacho dip in case that gets low, but you don't have to worry about that, since Mr. Green is in charge of snacks. Aphrodite? Are you listening?"

I couldn't get my gaze off the dance floor. The way the students were gliding around, it had to be covered with butter.

"You can't stand there," said Mr. Ripple, who must have crept up from behind. "Go around to the other side if you'd like punch." I smiled at him, and he looked surprised that it was me.

He turned to Miss Snipal. "Did you see the limousine? Eighth grade and someone sprang for a limo. It's crazy."

"Look at that couple," said Miss Snipal. "They're dancing too close."

"Oh, come on," said Mrs. Underwood. "I'll bet you were bumping it with the best of them at that age."

"Never," swore Miss Snipal.

"How about you, Aphrodite?" asked Mrs. Underwood. "You like to cut a rug? Surely there were dances at Harvard."

I checked the level of the punch bowl. "I suppose. I never had time for much other than my studies. Equations were my friends." Apart from Bernie the Squirrel and Alice, the cleaning lady, nobody ever came to visit me while I lived at Dr. Goode's house, and really, Bernie was in it for the Tootsie Rolls and Alice was there for the dirty sheets. Not that I wasn't invited to parties. There were lots of parties, big academic affairs where school officials in gray suits showed me off like I was the first loaf of sliced bread.

"Pooh pah! Look at those students," said Mrs. Underwood. Summer, Jordeen, and two older boys were thumping to the beat and laughing under the disco ball. "Can equations cut loose and live it up like that?" She sighed. "You've missed out on so much."

While Mrs. Underwood checked on the couples on the bleachers, I thought about what she'd said. All the time I was skipping grades so I could go to college early, it never occurred to me that I might have been missing out on something important in the process. Now I knew what I had given up: dress shopping, mugging for cameras, joking with girlfriends, and dancing with boys. It was a world I had never explored. But why shouldn't I? I decided to pretend I was a regular thirteen-year-old girl for the night and the students on the dance floor were my friends. I smiled until my lips began to ache.

The DJ put on a rock song that was so loud the refreshment table vibrated to the beat. I knew from a class I'd taken at Harvard that music played at such decibels could cause ear damage, and I wished I had anticipated the problem so I could have brought along some fitted earplugs. I looked under the table to see if there was anything I could use as a quick substitute. To my luck, there, right behind the chocolate syrup, was a large bag of miniature marshmallows. I used one of my manicured nails to poke a small hole in the bag and stuffed a mini-marshmallow in each ear.

Someone tapped me on the shoulder. "Professor Wigglesmith?" It was Adam.

"Would you like punch?" I asked, trying to be loud enough to be heard above the music. "It's got a bubbly kick."

"Yes, please," he said. I filled his cup and one for myself to propose a toast.

"To eighth-grade dances," I said, tapping our plastic cups. I gulped down the entire sugary concoction, slammed the cup against the table, and wiped the remains off my lips with the back of my hand.

Adam put a finger under his shirt collar and pulled. "Professor Wigglesmith?" he said. He cleared his throat. "I was wondering if . . ."

"What?" I asked, deciding the marshmallows had been a bad idea, but not knowing how to discreetly remove them.

"If you would like to dance?" he shouted.

On the dance floor, laughing silhouettes hipped, hopped, shook, and boogied. How would it feel to be one of them? I had already poured a dozen cups of punch and arranged them in front of the bowl in case

I got busy. Surely I wouldn't be missed for just a few minutes. "Yes," I shouted back. "I would love to dance."

The loud music cut off abruptly, and the DJ chirped, "All right you adolescent lovebirds, this slow one is coming at you from the hot new group, Once Bitten. It's 'Don't Walk Away.'"

I met Adam at the edge of the dance floor. He put a hand on the small of my back, and I reached up and perched both of my hands on his shoulders. He was so much taller than me that, with my arms stretched up, it must have looked like I was hanging on to the side of a mountain.

When the music started, we began to sway back and forth. I wasn't really sure how to dance, having only seen people do it on television, and I kept waiting for him to suddenly dip me or toss me up in the air. In reality, dancing for the first time is profoundly less dramatic. Basically, we wobbled like penguins as I stared at his shirt buttons and he gazed somewhere a foot over my head. Still, the rhythm of the music was quite mesmerizing. Once I closed my eyes, with the music muted by the marshmallows to a soft hum, it was enjoyable.

Albert Einstein once said that if you put your hand on a hot stove for a minute it will seem like an hour, but if you sit with a pretty girl for an hour it will seem like a minute. Never had his theory of relativity been more real to me. The music ended, but we continued to sway. When we pulled apart, I discovered we were the only couple on the floor. The rest of the students were mostly at the refreshment table, except for Timothy. He was standing next to me with a cup, saying something.

"What?" I asked as the DJ cranked up another loud song.

"I brought you punch," Timothy repeated loudly.

"Thank you," I mouthed, taking the cup. The odd smell hit me first. Then I noticed the strange deep reddish brown color and thick, chunky consistency to the liquid.

"What is this?" I yelled, holding it as far from my nose as possible.

"It's punch," Timothy shouted. "The bowl was empty, so I made more from the nottles yonder the stable." At least that's what it sounded like he said.

"Nottles yonder the stable?" I asked.

"I said, 'I made it from the bottles under the table.'"

My brain clicked to a mental image of the refreshment supplies: the Hawaiian Punch, orange juice, and ginger ale, but also the Hershey's chocolate syrup for the sundaes and Tabasco sauce and salsa for the nacho dip. "All of the bottles?" I shouted frantically.

"Sure," yelled Timothy. "Why not?"

That's when I saw the DJ, one hand suspended over the turntable, the other hand accepting a glass of punch from a student. I watched helplessly as he tilted the drink to his mouth and took in a gulp's worth. The DJ's cheeks inflated like overblown tires as he tried to keep the nasty concoction from being swallowed. The record-playing needle scratched across the turntable and the music died. While everyone stared, the DJ's eyes bulged and he raced around for a place to spit. He made it to a trash can, and the nasty punch shot from him like a gastrointestinal geyser.

"That's the most disgusting thing ever!" he cried.

Unfortunately, not all the others holding half-empty cups were able to locate places to safely dispose of their hideous brew. Even more unfortunately, nothing is more likely to make someone who hasn't had something obnoxious to drink throw up than the sight of others retching. Soon the dance floor was covered with random puddles of putrid punch.

Mr. Ripple rushed past me with a bucket and mop. "You!" he said. "What was in that punch?" He flopped the mop into a puddle and began pushing.

How could I respond? That I wasn't sure because I was too busy wobbling like a penguin with one of my students to notice the bowl had gone empty?

"You should know better than to leave your post," Mr. Ripple yelled. "I saw you dancing out there when you were supposed to be taking care of the refreshment table. Now look at the mess your irresponsible behavior caused."

Without the music blaring, his voice carried through the whole gym. Heat rushed to my face. He was right. This was my fault. I had no business being on the dance floor. I was not like the other thirteen-year-olds. I was never going to have a normal life, and I should have known better than to try to pretend. For once I had acted impulsively, putting my emotions over my sense of responsibility, and look what had happened.

The DJ came back and joked around with some students about having set off the punch-spewing rally. He looked around for a record to match the mood and, with a smile, placed one on the turntable. "Here's a song for all you kids out there with your tummies in a twist. It's by Shane Harper, but when you hear 'dance with me,' I want you to sing out 'puke with me.'"

The students started laughing and dancing again. A couple of them whom Mr. Ripple had conscripted into janitorial duty even started to dance with the mops. Whenever the song hit its refrain, the students all yelled out "puke with me" like it was the funniest thing in the world.

Mr. Ripple turned and glared at me. I didn't need to take the mini-marshmallows out of my ears to hear his message. Miss Snipal replaced me at the punch bowl. My services were no longer needed, and it was time for me to go. I drifted away from the dance floor and snuck toward the exit door. One push on the metal door and I was outside, alone in the darkness.

The sky was vast and starless. I dashed to the front of the building, making it to where the limo was parked. I wanted to go home, but if I took the limo it would leave the other girls stranded. I had a sudden urge to throw my shoes off and run. I would flip them high into the air, like Mindy does with her baton, and run home so fast that I wouldn't hear them land. Home was where everything was orderly and predictable, from the 316 ceramic wall tiles in the bathroom to the 1,458 bristles in my toothbrush. Maybe the comfort I got from predictability was the reason why, as Mindy had pointed out, I always did what was expected of me.

I had never deliberately disobeyed a rule in my life—until tonight. The time I glued the chairs to the students' rear ends to try to get them to listen, the incident when I took them to the pool hall to learn about angles but didn't get written permission slips beforehand, those were just innocent mistakes. Leaving the punch bowl unattended so I could go dancing was something I had done intentionally. It was all so confusing. Sometimes I felt like a teacher pretending to be a student and other times I felt like a student pretending to be a teacher.

Headlights appeared out of the darkness. The windows to a sedan were open, and I could hear loud party music blaring as it sped by. The car swerved, and the driver had to regain control and proceed at a slower pace.

Control, I thought. *I have to stay in control.* I found my cell phone where I'd left it in the limousine and called my mother. Fortunately, she was used to dropping everything for emergencies without demanding details.

"I'll be right there," Mother said.

The drive home took forever. The night had turned chilly, and I removed Mindy's shoes and held my feet near the car's floor heater.

"Mother," I said, "I want to ask you a question. But I don't want you to answer it as a parent, just as a person."

"I'll try," she said.

"Do you ever feel like you're just pretending to be yourself, and if you really had to be yourself you wouldn't know who to be?"

"What a strange question," she replied.

I tried to gather my thoughts better. "If I hadn't skipped all those grades and gone to Harvard, if I had stayed in regular school instead—what do you think I would be like?"

"Are you having regrets?"

I went to push the bangs out of my eyes, but they weren't there. "I don't know, I said.

"Is this about the phone call from Harvard?" Mother asked.

"What?"

"On the answering machine. It was Dr. Goode. He said that the board of trustees read about your teaching success in an article in *The New York Times*. Now that you've collected enough field data, Harvard wants you back."

By morning, there were four messages on the machine.

"Why does everyone look so serious?" Father asked as he came into the kitchen for breakfast. He grabbed a cereal bowl and poured in milk.

"Aphrodite is having second thoughts about taking the position at Harvard," said Mother.

"I didn't say that, exactly." I scraped my oatmeal into the trash can and placed the bowl in the dishwasher. "I'm just not sure I'm ready to go back. I mean, how do I know I've really proven my theory until my students win the Great Math Showdown? Besides, how would they feel if I suddenly left them?"

"Maybe you should talk to Mindy," Mother suggested. "The two of you have been spending a lot of time together. She could let you know how the other students would feel."

It was a great idea, right up there with the high-waisted plumber's pants Mother made for herself to avoid plumber's butt. A heart-to-heart chat with Mindy would be just the thing to help me decide if I should take the position at Harvard right away or stay at Carnegie Middle School. So many things had happened at the dance; I was grateful to have a friend I could discuss them with. I dialed Mindy's home number six times, but getting no answer, decided to walk to the beauty shop.

Tiffany's House of Beauty & Nails smelled like polish remover and hair dye. I knew the chemicals could

kill brain cells, but I liked the smell because it reminded me of getting ready for the dance.

"So the beauty queen graces us with a visit," said
Tiffany with a wink, admiring the hairdo she'd created
for me. I had slept sitting up all night so as not to ruin it.

"Hello, Mrs. Loft. Is Mindy around?"

"She's been up in her room sulking since she got
back last night. Says she doesn't want to talk about it."

"Would it be all right if I went up to say hello?"

"Be my guest," she said. "Remind her she's got an
appointment to do a set of nails in an hour—whether
she's in the mood or not."

By the time I got to the top of the steps leading to
the Lofts' apartment, I was positive that a nice chat
with Mindy would make everything better. Foolish me.

16 Mindy Shows Her True Color

"Okay, okay," I hollered when I heard the knock on the door. Then I made the mistake of glancing in the mirror on my way to answer it. I was wearing the same dirty bathrobe and pajamas I had slept in, if you want to call all that lousy tossing and turning I did the night before sleep. The ringlets were still in my hair, but they were totally limp and frizzy. Yesterday's makeup was smudged like war paint across my face.

I cracked open the door, trying to see who it was, without letting them see me. It was the totally last person in the universe that I wanted to be there—Dytee. "What do *you* want?"

She stumbled backwards a little. "Mindy?"

"No," I said. "I'm the creature from the green lagoon."

"I think you mean the creature from the black lagoon."

"It's my lagoon. I can make it any color I want."

She smiled, confusing my irritation for humor. "May I come in?"

"What for? Is there something you want to steal in here?" Before she could answer, I turned and headed off to the bathroom to wash the makeup off my face. I poured warm water into my hands and scrubbed until it all ran down the drain. Meanwhile, Dytee had let herself in and appeared beside me.

"Is something wrong?" she asked.

I patted my face dry so hard with the towel that it scratched. "Wrong?" I yelled. "How can you even ask after what you did to me?"

"I'm afraid I'm a bit flummoxed," she said, shrinking back. "What specifically did I do?"

"Don't play sweet and stupid," I said, throwing my dirty towel at her image in the mirror. "You totally know what you did—you boyfriend stealer—so drop the innocent routine. *I* like Adam, and *I* have dibs on him. You don't go dancing with someone when someone else has dibs. You're an eggs Benedict!"

"I think you mean Benedict Arnold."

"Don't try to tell me what I mean. The entire eighth

grade saw you, and everybody knows I like him. Do you realize how embarrassed I was? Not only did he not ask me to dance, he asked you—of all people!"

"This is a misunderstanding," Dytee said. "Adam and I don't like each other that way."

I pushed her toward the front door. "If you expect me to believe that, you are treeing up the wrong bark. You've had a crush on him since day one. If you ask me it's disgusting, because you're supposed to be a teacher, and you shouldn't be hitting on your students."

"I don't think I would even know *how* to hit on a student," she said, "even if I wanted to."

"So you don't think Adam is good enough for you?"

"That's not what I meant."

"See," I said. "You do like him."

"He's nice person," she said. "Look, maybe I should come back at another time."

"That's right," I said. "Just run out on me, like you did at the dance. First you ignored me the whole time you were there. Then you stole my dibfriend. Then you ruined the dance with your stupid vomit punch and snuck off without even saying good-bye."

"When did I ignore you?" she asked.

"What? Are you really going to pretend you didn't

hear me call your name a half-dozen times when you walked by me without an acknowledgment?"

She sighed, looked me directly in the eyes, and said, "I had marshmallows in my ears."

It was the most stupid, unbelievable thing I had ever heard. "Here's a lesson for you called Friendship one-o-one," I told her. "First, friends don't lie to each other. Second, they don't steal the boyfriends of other friends who have dibs. Third, they don't ignore each other at dances. And fourth, they don't do stupid stuff that louses up the dance for everyone else in the school. It was completely ruined! Everybody got so out of control that they had to shut down the dance early and send us all home." I folded my arms dramatically. "Now, leave."

She slunk out, and then turned as if to say something. I quickly slammed the door. The bang was so satisfying I decided to do it again. I flung the door back open. She was still frozen in place. "I wish you'd never come to Carnegie Middle School!" I yelled, and for good measure I added, "Why don't you go back to Harvard where you belong?"

I slammed the door even harder, and listened for Dytee's footsteps. After a minute of silence, I flung the door back open, but she was gone.

+ - + - +

I let Dytee stew that night, but I never can stay mad long-term, because I always feel better after I tell someone off. By morning I had already decided to forgive her. I didn't really want to lose her friendship. Spending time with Dytee was different than with other girls. She was always willing to listen, didn't shy away from serious subjects, and helped me without expecting anything in return. Of course, she shouldn't have danced with Adam. A good friend would have realized I had a crush on him and encouraged him to dance with me instead. And, as much as it did sound like the weird kind of thing she might actually do, a good friend wouldn't stuff marshmallows in her ears when she knew her good friend was at the same dance and might want to talk to her.

Thinking about how a good friend should act made me realize why I had overreacted and turned into the creature from the whatever-color lagoon about the whole thing: I *did* consider Dytee a good friend, the first really good friend I had ever had. And when a good friend does something that disappoints you, it hurts. All of this occurred to me just as I was about to step into math class.

"Good morning," said Miss Snipal. She was sitting with her rear leaned against Dytee's desk. She had her bucket of balls next to her and was tossing one up and down in her hand. I glanced around to make sure I was in the right room.

"Glad you could join us. As I've been telling your classmates, I will be filling in again until a new math teacher can be found."

I took my seat. "Where's Professor Wigglesmith?"

"Did she catch the flu?" asked Keisha.

"Is she in trouble?" asked Adam.

"Did she get punched by the punch?" asked Timothy.

The room erupted in questions, and Miss Snipal had to throw a half-dozen Ping-Pong balls to shut us up. "Professor Wigglesmith has returned to Harvard," she said. "It was never her intention to stay long-term. I suppose she had enough and left."

"She wouldn't do that," said Roland.

"But she has," said Miss Snipal.

Bobby raised his hand. "What about us?" he asked. "How can we pass math without her? She's the only teacher who made it so I could understand."

"And what about the Great Math Showdown?" asked Roland. "How are we supposed to win without her help?"

"We can't do it without her," Hunter said.

"We're gonna get slaughtered," said LeeAnn, "in front of the whole school."

"My job is to take over this math class," replied Miss Snipal. "Not to volunteer my after-school time for a math contest. Professor Wigglesmith should never have entered you in that competition if she didn't intend on sticking it through until the end."

That's when it hit me, like a baton to the noggin. The last thing I had said to Dytee was that she should go back to Harvard. She *had* intended on sticking it through to the end—until I told her not to.

"I don't believe it," Adam said. "She wouldn't walk out on us, not without even saying good-bye."

"Do you see her here? No. She's gone. Kaput. Finished. Now, let's move on. Who can tell me where you left off in the book?"

Eugenia raised her hand. "But why?" she asked. "Why did Professor Wigglesmith go back to Harvard?"

"Really," said Miss Snipal. "If you had a choice between spending your time with Ivy League brains or surrounded by boneheads, which would you choose?"

"She's not like that," said Roland, "and we don't call ourselves boneheads anymore. Professor Wigglesmith says anyone can be a math wiz." A Ping-Pong ball landed in his open mouth.

"Wizzes fizzes," said Miss Snipal. "Why would she go around inflating expectations like that? Second strings are better off when they own up to their limitations. If Professor Wigglesmith led you to believe otherwise, she's a bonehead, too."

After all Dytee had done to help us, hearing Miss Snipal say those rotten things about her made me want to throw something, too. A good friend would defend her friend's honor. A Ping-Pong ball rolled near my desk. I thought about the distance from Miss Snipal to me, how many desks were between us, and the probability that another student might stand or put a hand up. Then I checked out the wall to the side of the blackboard where Miss Snipal stood and thought about angles. "Professor Wigglesmith is not a bonehead," I muttered, "and neither are we." I grabbed the ball and pitched it against the side wall. The ball bounced against the blackboard, ricocheted off, and whacked Miss Snipal in the back of the head.

"Why you little . . . Who threw that ball?"

The kids in front of me ducked, and Miss Snipal lobbed a ball straight at me. But Roland reached over and caught it and fired it back at her. Suddenly, it was a Ping-Pong riot. Kids were scooping up the balls and throwing them back at Miss Snipal faster than she could return them. When her bucket was empty, Miss Snipal raced out the door and down the hall, fleeing a shower of bouncing white balls. We hooted and high-fived one another for what seemed like ten minutes, and then the room suddenly went silent.

"What do we do now?" asked Eugenia.

I tossed my tattered math book on my desk and cracked it open. "The best we can," I said. Maybe it was because I didn't appreciate her like I should have when she was around, always worrying instead about what the other kids would think if we were caught being friends. Maybe it was because Dytee had made me realize that if I worked hard enough, even I could be a math wiz, or at least wizish. Or maybe it was because I knew I was responsible for making her feel like she wasn't welcome and sending her back to Harvard. Whatever the reason, I knew that it was up to me now to somehow try to keep the math team together. "We're going to that competition, with or without Professor Wigglesmith, and we're going to prove that we're not losers."

"Do you think we still have a chance?" asked Eugenia.

"I know we do," I said. "Professor Wigglesmith

believed in us, and now it's time for us to believe in ourselves."

I used my competition voice to make it extra-convincing. What else could I say? What I really felt—that without Dytee we were doomed? It was my fault she had left. The last thing I had said to her was "Why don't you go back to Harvard where you belong?" and she had. Because of me and my big mouth, she was gone. It was weird, because up until that moment I hadn't even realized I cared if we won the Great Math Showdown, but now it felt like it was the most important thing in my life.

When I really thought about it, everything I had been doing up until then, I had been doing for myself. The only reason I'd joined the math team was to try to get Adam to like me so I could have a cool boyfriend. The only reason I stayed with it was because I liked hanging out with Dytee, even if I pretended otherwise so I could stay popular. But now that I had made a mess of it, I didn't feel bad for myself. I felt bad for the other kids in the class, especially Adam, not because he was cute, but because I knew how much winning the Great Math Showdown meant to him. What else could I say? After what I had done, I owed it to them to try.

The next day, Miss Snipal did not show for class, but Principal DeGuy did. His arms were folded across his chest. "Because of your conduct, Miss Snipal refuses to return. Frankly, after what happened yesterday, I don't blame her." He scanned the room accusingly. "There's not a substitute within a fifty-mile radius who will put up with this class."

I imagined a dingy office somewhere where teachers stood in long lines applying for new jobs. The walls of the office were plastered with posters with our class photo on them. "Are those 'Wanted' posters?" a math teacher asks. "Look closer," another replies. "Those are '*Not* Wanted' posters."

"Why can't we have Professor Wigglesmith?" asked Keisha as she tied her pigtails together in a knot.

"Nobody would love that more than me," said Principal DeGuy, "but she's gone for good. Problem is, we can't have a class without a teacher. You may all have to take incompletes and finish up your math credit during summer school at a different middle school, unless you want to repeat the eighth grade."

"You're joking," cried Roland.

"Holy sardine and liverwurst sandwiches," said

Principal DeGuy. "Does it sound like I'm joking?"

"I don't want to repeat eighth grade," said Salvador. He pulled off his eyeglasses and ran his arm across his eyes.

"You should have thought about that before pummeling Miss Snipal with Ping-Pong balls."

Adam sat up. "How will I tell my parents?"

"That's called a consequence," said Principal De-Guy, "and it's a direct result of your action."

"Don't take it out on them," I said. I stood and took a big gulp of breath. "It's not their fault she left. I'm the one who told Professor Wigglesmith to go back to Harvard."

Principal DeGuy's mouth dropped open, then Roland's, then Hunter's. Then it spread all across the room like a game of dental dominoes. "But why?" Principal DeGuy asked.

I wanted to explain that I didn't think she would take me seriously, that I was mad at her because she danced with Adam, and I thought she knew I liked Adam, and that I had called dibs, but I forgot that she wasn't used to things like dibs. I wanted to explain that when I heard the music and saw them, I only thought about my own feelings, and then when she came to see me I was mean and hateful because I expected her to be a good friend to me even though I wasn't a good friend to her, and now I realized what a jerk I was. But if I did explain everything, maybe they would feel a tiny bit sorry for me and I didn't deserve that.

So, what I said was: "Because I'm a jerk."

"I will deal with you after class, young lady," said Principal DeGuy.

I plopped back into my seat and felt my skin burning with embarrassment.

"What if we stay here and keep working on our math?" asked Adam. "If we do the assignments and hold regular classes, why can't we get the credit?"

"Without a teacher?" asked Principal DeGuy.

Roland asked, "If we teach ourselves, and pass the test at the end, why not?"

"With no teacher, who's going to give you the test?"

"The Great Math Showdown," I said. They looked at me like I was a monster, the ugly kind that crawls out of a swamp, not the cute kind that eats cookies, but what I had to say was too important to let that stop me. "That could be our test. If we were to win the math competition, it would prove we should pass."

"She's right," said Adam. "That could work."

"I know you don't like the situation," said Principal DeGuy, "but be realistic."

Eugenia raised her hand. "If we went to the Great Math Showdown but we didn't win," she said, "then we could still go to summer school. What's the harm in letting us try?"

"Holy pink slip! Losing my job, that's what the harm is. The school board does not allow students to teach themselves."

"What the school board doesn't know can't hurt it," said Roland.

"Please," pleaded Eugenia, who was so determined, she forgot to raise her hand.

Principal DeGuy was weakening. "I admire your spunk. I wish I could say yes."

A tiny voice from the back of the room spoke so softly you could hardly hear it. "We just want a chance." It was Bobby DeGuy. The kids turned to look at him. "Please, Dad, just give us a chance."

Principal DeGuy dropped his arms and arched his eyebrows. He went over to Bobby and put his hand on his shoulder.

"Listen, son. I'm proud you want to try. But even if I let you enter the competition, how can you beat the honors and academic math classes?"

"Maybe we won't," said Bobby. "But you're always telling me that I should stick up for myself, that even if

I am small for my age, and got held back in third grade, I'm just as good. I want my chance. Isn't failing better than being afraid to try?"

Principal DeGuy sighed. "Okay, I give," he said. "Never in my twenty-two years in this school district have I met a group of students with a greater desire to learn. Who am I to try to stop you?"

We jumped out of our seats and cheered.

"But," yelled Principal DeGuy over the roar, "there will be rules!"

We sat.

Principal DeGuy went to the front of the room and selected a long white piece of chalk. "First," he said, "you will continue with the assignments in your math book. You will grade one another's homework, and then leave it in a folder at the end of each class. Adam Boyce, since you are the captain of the math team, Professor Wigglesmith must have put a lot of faith in you. Therefore, you will be in charge of making sure your classmates turn in their homework, without cheating. I will check every night."

"You can count on me," said Adam.

Principal DeGuy continued. "Second, if anyone asks who is in charge of this classroom, tell them I am.

Needs to be somebody's name on the paperwork—it might as well be mine.

"Third, you are all on the honor system. I cannot run back and forth checking on this class. Do your work, study, no troublemaking. Roland Geruch, any disciplinary problems you report to me immediately. Understand?"

"Yes, sir," said Roland, with a military salute.

"Fourth, your grades will be determined by Professor Wigglesmith's records and by your performance at the Great Math Showdown.

"Fifth." Principal DeGuy snapped the chalk in two. "No half efforts. This is your chance. Remember, you asked for it. Any questions?"

Timothy raised his hand. "I have one. What did they call the Roman war hero who was good at math?"

The whole class groaned in unison.

"General Calculus."

Principal DeGuy went over to Timothy's desk and leaned in close. "That's a good one," he said. "Now here's one for you. What did they call the eighth grader who didn't know when to stop joking around?"

"What?" asked Timothy.

"A seventh grader," he answered.

After Principal DeGuy left, I became invisible. Everyone was so mad they ignored me. In one minute, I was demoted from the most to the least popular girl in class. Worse, I knew I deserved it. I wondered if things were going any better for Dytee. *At least at Harvard,* I thought, *Dytee will be surrounded by people who appreciate her.*

17 Aphrodite Resumes the Dog and Pony Show

In front of Harvard's University Hall is a statue nicknamed "The Statue of Three Lies." Although its inscription reads "John Harvard/Founder/1638," the statue was modeled after someone else, the university was founded by someone else, and the correct date of its founding was two years prior. When I looked at the statue after returning to Harvard, it reminded me of my own lie, the one I'd told Dr. Goode when I called and told him I wanted to come back.

"Hello," I said to a lonely pigeon on a bench. "Are you hungry?" I took out a granola bar and tossed crumbs on the ground. I was crossing Harvard Yard, headed toward the administration building for a Mensa meeting. Mensa is an organization for people whose intelligence has tested in the top two percent in the world, and once a month, local members meet at Harvard for networking. I stopped on the bench to watch the pigeon peck up the tidbits. As soon as it was done, it flew away.

It was May, and undergraduate students were playing touch football in the grass. Suddenly, a football whizzed by within inches of my head. A young man with a goatee and dimples raced toward me.

"Sorry!" he yelled. He picked up the ball and threw it back. It formed a spiraling arch and was caught by a busty young woman in a tight brown sweater. The man plopped down next to me. "Are you okay? I didn't mean to scare you. I've been throwing wide lately. Hey, you're the little math genius kid, aren't you?"

"I'm a professor now."

"Right," he said. "Cool."

I didn't know what else to say. The ability I had to talk with boys in my class at Carnegie Middle School had evaporated on the wings of my flight back to Boston.

"Well, I better get back in there," the young man said. "See you around."

I watched the undergraduates laughing and playing for so long I was late.

+ - + - +

"There you are," said Dr. Goode. He was a reserved man with broad shoulders and a slight Caribbean accent. "I've got someone I want you to meet." We were in the same stuffy room where the Mensa group always met. I had been back only two weeks and the dog and pony show had already resumed.

Dr. Goode handed me seltzer water and led me forward. The room seemed dark, even though every bulb in the giant chandelier was shining. I silently counted the bulbs and figured the wattage. It *should* have generated enough light. Why did it feel so gloomy?

Dr. Goode brought me to a small group. A woman in a pin-striped suit looked down and nodded politely at me. She had slightly graying hair pulled back in a barrette like the style I had returned to. After we were formally introduced, the woman's eyes lit up and her hand shot out. "I read about you in *The New York Times*," she said. Her strong handshake practically lifted me off the floor.

"Professor Wigglesmith's talents are being put to very good use," Dr. Goode said. "She's working on the Millennium Prize Problems."

"Are you making much progress?" asked a stout man with a thick mustache, a banker whom I recognized from previous meetings.

The listeners waited and I blushed. Since returning, I hadn't felt like doing equations. The meeting was going from bad to worse. Perhaps if I added some levity, like Timothy always did when things got rough.

"Would you like to hear a joke?" I asked.

Dr. Goode looked startled. "I really don't think—"

"It's a math joke. You see, Albert Einstein was always lecturing about his theories, and after a number of years of him giving the same lecture, his driver, who always sat in the back and waited for him, said, 'I've heard that same lecture so many times I'll bet I could give it.' So Einstein—most people don't know this but he had a great sense of humor—said, 'Okay. At our next stop, you give the lecture and I'll sit in the audience.' The driver did, and he did a fine job, but after the lecture someone from the audience asked him a really hard question. Without flinching, he responded, 'That one's so easy I'm going to let my driver answer it.'"

They stared at me as if I had grown an extra head.

I chugged down my seltzer water. "Would you excuse me? I need to get another drink." I crept past the bar and left. "What's wrong with me?" I asked myself as I walked to my room.

A plain brown package was waiting for me in front of my door. It was from my parents. I opened it and fished below the crinkled newspapers. Something felt soft: Hershey Bear. There was a note from my mother.

Dear Aphrodite,
Hermy didn't want you to be alone, so he asked me
to send Hershey Bear.
We all miss you very much.
With Love, Mother

Tears pooled in my eyes. I had left Hershey Bear with Hermy so he wouldn't miss me, but Hermy knew I would need the bear more than he did. Homesickness was an ache inside my chest. I wanted to be back in my own dining room happily dodging squash. I wanted to hang out with the gang at the Carnegie Diner for math team practice. What were my students working on in class? I hoped they weren't allowing themselves to fall behind.

Dr. Goode had wanted me to return to Harvard immediately, and I had done so without a word to the class. After what had happened at the dance and with

Mindy, I felt like I didn't belong. Mr. Ripple was mad at me for leaving the refreshment stand unattended, Mindy was mad at me for dancing with Adam, and the students probably were mad at me for ruining their dance. It was strange, but even though she was the one who told me I should leave, I missed Mindy most.

Maybe it was the way I'd left. Without a proper good-bye, how could I get on with things? I tried to shake the feeling. I could not change the past, and it would do no good to dwell there. I had to be practical. No matter how much I missed Carnegie Middle School, Harvard was my life now.

18 Mindy Gets the Short End of the Baton

I must have thrown that baton a zillion times, but it just wouldn't fly straight. Each time it came down crooked and whapped me somewhere, or I would trip over my own foot and splatter onto the ground like a cartoon character.

"Gracefully," Miss Brenda said as I chased after the baton. "Remember, if you drop a baton, always retrieve it *gracefully*."

I felt the sore spot on my head. It was hard to fake grace with cartoon stars circling your noggin, but I put on my show smile and continued my routine. Miss Brenda already had started packing for the closing of the studio, and the posters and team trophies were in boxes. The Baton Barn was starting to look like an old warehouse that should be torn down, and I had to act like it was okay because Miss Brenda said I would "land on my feet somehow."

Buster Wigglesmith caught my gaze and waved at me from the parent waiting area. Dytee had been gone two weeks, but her dad still insisted on driving me to baton lessons. It beat having to ride my bike, but I felt bad about her family being so nice to me after what a creep I had been to Dytee.

The new routine for the Twirlcrazy Grand Championship involved two batons and lots of gymnastics. Miss Brenda had somehow convinced me to agree to choreograph the routine to Michael Jackson's song "Bad," which wasn't exactly cheering me up. I tried to focus on putting more speed into my butterfly twirl, but my mind kept wandering to the Great Math Showdown.

Even with all the studying I had been doing at home on my own, I felt like I was still the worst student in math class, but I hadn't been able to convince anyone to take my place, so the team was stuck with me. Each team had to submit a list of nine members. The first six (Adam, Eugenia, Roland, Salvador, Keisha, and LeeAnn) would answer questions, and the remaining three (Bobby, Hunter, and I) would be the alternates.

I wasn't worried as much about losing as I was about

not having enough team members to play. Even though we kept meeting at the Carnegie Diner for practice, it was harder to understand the math concepts without Dytee's help. Hunter was discouraged, and LeeAnn missed a lot of practices, coming up with lame excuses about having to do things like wash her cat. I suspected she was lying just to get out of it, but I put on my show smile and didn't say a word. After all, I wasn't exactly in the best position to complain about how other kids were handling the situation.

The team still hadn't forgiven me for telling Dytee to leave. Only Adam had somehow gotten over it. "Even though what you did was mean, it took guts to confess to Principal DeGuy so he wouldn't blame the rest of the class for her wanting to go," said Adam.

I didn't know how to respond. "Thanks, I guess."

"Really," said Adam. "I used to think you were one of those shallow, popular girls who only cared about herself, but I was wrong about you."

"No," I said. "You were right. But people can change."

Later, I filled him in on all the reasons I blew up at Dytee, partly because he asked, but mostly because I didn't want to keep it all bottled up inside and I missed having someone to talk to since Dytee was gone. Adam told me he had asked Dytee to dance to find out what Harvard was like, since that was his dream school, but when the DJ switched to the slow song Adam was so worried about stepping on her feet he didn't say anything.

"Straight," ordered Miss Brenda, holding my arm by the wrist and pressing against the elbow. "If you want to win you must be perfect."

Over and over again, I performed my two-baton freestyle solo routine. The music pulled Dytee's dad and brother over from the waiting area and gave me a reason to do my best. Each time I caught a baton, Hermy squealed and yelled, "Again!" When I did my back flip at the end, they burst into applause. I took a deep bow, imagining I was already wearing the first place medallion.

"Hold up," said Miss Brenda as we were on our way out. "I really am getting old—I almost forgot to tell you. There's been a schedule change in the competition. The two-baton solos have been moved from Wednesday to Thursday."

I nearly choked on my after-practice Doritos.

"That gives you an extra day of practice. We'll meet at the same time, but on—"

"Thursday," I said with a shudder. The odds had to be 365 to 1—the same night as the Great Math Showdown.

When I got home, I got out a piece of paper and drew a line down the middle. On one side I wrote *Baton Competition* and on the other side I wrote *Math Showdown*. I figured I would list the best reasons for going to each, and that would help me decide.

It reminded me of the day Mom said I was old enough to dye my hair if I wanted, but I couldn't decide if I should be a blond or a redhead. So I dyed one-half of my hair blond and the other half of my hair red. Then, when I still couldn't decide, I dyed the blond side red and the red side blond, figuring that would somehow give me one color that was a blend of both. Here's a beauty tip—don't try it. What you'll get is a totally splotchy mess and some bald spots, although if you're lucky enough to have an expert beautician in the family, you can get it dyed back to something close to your natural color.

The thing about messing up my hair was that it didn't hurt anyone but me, same as if I skipped the Twirlcrazy Grand Championship. But if I didn't go to the Great Math Showdown, it would be like pouring multicolored hair dye on every kid on the math team.

I took a folding chair out to the front of the beauty shop so I could get some fresh air while I thought. It was dark, but the light from the beauty shop lit up the area. "Fingernails clogged with manure, come in for a manicure," the sign said.

The door opened and the happy sounds of women chatting flowed out. Even though people said she was ditzy, everybody loved my mom. It made me feel a little jealous, but glad for her, too. I mean, if she had a big decision to make that was really important to her, she wouldn't have any problem finding someone to listen and help her figure out what to do. Who could I call?

Veronica, Jordeen, and Summer never understood why I bothered with the math team. They thought the other kids in my math class were all worthless idiots. I could almost hear their reaction if I went to them for advice:

"Your twirl thingy is at the same time as that stupid math contest?" Veronica would say. "Great. That means you've got a good excuse to skip the Great Math Showdown and you won't have to embarrass yourself in front of the whole school by coming in last place."

"But I'm the one who told the team we should try to go for it," I'd say.

Then Jordeen would add, "You don't owe those losers anything. Do what you want to do."

But doing what I wanted to do, and only thinking about myself, is what got me here—sitting alone in the dark. It's funny, in a sad way, because it's the opposite of what happened to Dytee. Thinking only about how other people felt and doing what other people wanted her to do is what made her listen to me and go back to Harvard. It's almost like we have the same problem, only switched around, and that's when I realized that the best person to call about my big decision was Dytee. I just hoped she would forgive me for being so rotten to her and take my call.

I remembered her talking about living in Dr. Goode's house while she went to school there, which gave me the bright idea to call her mom and ask for the number. Calling Dytee would give me a chance to make sure she knew I was sorry, too. I couldn't believe I hadn't thought to do it sooner.

"This is the Goode residence," a woman answered. She had a weird kind of accent, like she was from another country.

"Can I speak to Aphrodite Wigglesmith?"

"Who may I say is calling?" the woman asked.

"This is Mindy Loft. I was one of her students at Carnegie Middle School."

The phone went quiet, like the woman had put her hand over the receiver, and it took a few seconds before she spoke again. "I'm sorry, but she's not available."

"Can I leave her a message?"

More silence, and then I heard the woman say softly, as if whispering to someone else, "It's one of those children from the test class."

"Not again," said the man. Then there was a clunk like somebody dropped the phone, and the man was talking to me directly. When I asked him if I could talk to Dytee, he said, "She's working and can't be disturbed."

"It's okay," I said. "I wanted to ask her something, but I realize now that I already know the answer."

After I hung up, I pulled the piece of paper with the line down the middle from my pocket. Once, I told Dytee that I thought she was the worst teacher I ever had, but it turned out she was the best. She taught me what it meant to be a real friend and to be part of a team. Sometimes it means making sacrifices for other people. That night, sitting in the dark, looking up at the stars, I felt like I'd finally put two and two together. I drew a line through the words *Baton Competition*, and circled *Math Showdown*. It was the least boneheaded decision I had ever made.

19 Aphrodite Gets the Fast Cab out of Beantown

Here's a test you can do if you're a teacher and you want to see if students are really listening. While you're lecturing, slip over to your desk, pull a banana out of your lunch, place it on your head, and wait to see if anyone notices.

"Remember to turn in your proofs by Friday," I told a class of yawning Harvard sophomores as the dismissal bell rang after early-morning class. "And check the schedule for the time of the final exam."

The students raced off. I took the banana off my head and slumped in my seat. It wasn't their fault. Dr. Goode thought it might help cheer me if I guest lectured a few classes, but I just couldn't stop feeling sad and tired all the time, particularly this morning.

It was May 23, the date of the Great Math Show-down.

I went to my room to lie down, changing from my gray suit into my pink sweats and bunny slippers. The box that Hershey Bear had come in was still sitting on the floor next to my bed. I opened it and smelled the crumpled newspaper.

I selected a page and straightened it. It was from the *Carnegie Signal Item*. There was an advertisement for Wigglesmith Plumbing, and a notice about the school lunch menu. I picked up another piece and uncrumpled it. "Local Girls Set to Compete in Baton Competition," an article said. It was about how the girls from Miss Brenda's Baton Barn were going to the Twirlcrazy Grand Championship.

Mindy was finally going to have her day and I would not be there to cheer her on. At least I should call her and wish her good luck. Maybe enough time had passed that she wouldn't be mad at me anymore. Maybe she could have the competition videotaped so I could watch it here.

I reached for the phone, but stopped myself. When I first got back to Harvard, I'd talked about my students at Carnegie Middle School so much that Dr. Goode said he was concerned that I had formed an unhealthy attachment with my research subjects. He suggested a temporary ban from contact with my former students. Even though it didn't feel right, I had gone along with it, neither taking their calls nor calling them. I knew Dr. Goode would frown on me calling Mindy, maybe even get angry, but I grabbed the phone anyway and dialed Mindy's home phone number. When there was no answer, I tried the beauty shop.

"Tiffany's House of Beauty and Nails," answered a strange male voice. "Home of the so-bright hi-light special."

"May I speak with Mindy, please?"

"She's not here."

"Tiffany, please?"

"Up to her elbows in a two-hour hair extension. You want an appointment?"

"No."

"Want to hear our specials? 'Beauty denied is happiness delayed. For twenty-nine ninety-nine get unlimited braids.' Or how about this one: 'Hair that's too straight is hair you can hate. For forty-three eighty-four, make it curly galore.'"

"This is Aphrodite Wigglesmith. Would you please tell Mrs. Loft that it's important?"

I heard the phone hitting the appointment desk and the soft 1970s love songs that play when you're on hold.

"How you doing, kiddo?" Mindy's mom sounded happy to hear from me.

"I'm okay, Mrs. Loft. I wanted to wish Mindy good luck at the Twirlcrazy Grand Championship."

"You and me, both. But the fact is, Mindy's decided not to compete."

I tried to keep my voice from sounding too frantic. "But with the Baton Barn closing, this may be her last competition. She can't just give up on her dream."

"Don't I know it?" said Mrs. Loft. "But the Twirlcrazy Grand Championship and the Great Math Showdown are on the same day and Mindy's made up her mind. If the math contest means that much to her, there's no way I'm going to talk her out of it. I would think you'd be happy. You're the one that got her involved in all of that math stuff."

Mindy was giving up her last chance to win a baton trophy so she could help the math team. The team that I had walked out on, she was seeing through to the end.

"Look," said Mrs. Loft. "I've got a half-head of extensions I've got to get back to. It was nice talking to you."

After I hung up, I tried to focus on my equations, but I couldn't stop thinking about Mindy and the rest of the team. Statistically, my students didn't stand a chance. After all, the collective IQs of the other teams were higher, and without my help the remedial class probably hadn't been making the most of its study time.

Anyone could be a math wiz. That's what I had set out to prove. But did I really believe it? Maybe I only wanted to believe it, because if anyone could be a math wiz, then anyone could be like me, and that meant I wasn't really so different from everyone else. Was that why I had tried so hard to prove my theory? So I could feel better about myself? Had I stopped to consider how my students might feel if they lost?

I checked my watch. It was a little past noon in Boston. The Great Math Showdown started at 6:00 p.m. in Carnegie, Pennsylvania. No matter how impulsive it seemed, I couldn't let it start without me. That gave me just six hours to travel nearly six hundred miles.

I dialed the number for an airport taxi.

20 Mindy Faces the Lions

*N*ot only were Adam and I the first to show for the competition, we were so early that we were drafted into setting up chairs on the sides of the gym that didn't have bleachers. Mom had closed the beauty shop so she could come, and she waved at me from the top of the bleachers. She wore a T-shirt she had made herself. The back of it said: *If your hair is mad from too much teasing, a trip to Tiffany's is extra pleasing,* but the front simply said: *Go, Mindy!*

"We're expecting a crowd," said Mr. Ripple. "Channel Four News is going to be here."

I lost three pounds sweating as I waited for the team to arrive. Eugenia came wearing her rattiest sweater and carrying a box of tissues to wipe her red nose. "I think it's the flu," she said dramatically. "But I couldn't let the team down."

Bobby and Salvador arrived at the same time and announced that Hunter had chickened out. Keisha hurried over, fumbling with a stack of yellow pads and number-two pencils. "Is everybody here?" she asked. She was wearing green ribbons in her pigtails, which were braided extra tight.

"Not yet," said Adam. "But let's start getting ready." Our group went over to the table with the green tablecloth. Adam, Eugenia, Salvador, and Kiesha each took a seat, pad, and pencil, as the bleachers began to fill.

The table to the right of us had a brown tablecloth and was for the members of the academic math team. The table lined up to the right of that one, covered in a yellow tablecloth, was for the honors/gifted and talented team. As we waited for the rest of our team, all six seats at each of the other tables were filled.

I kept my eye on the entrance. If LeeAnn and Roland didn't show, our team wouldn't have any backup in case there was a problem. Worse, it would mean we alternates couldn't just sit in the special section in case we were needed; Bobby and I would have to play.

A chubby third grader with a crew cut and Sponge-

Bob SquarePants T-shirt raced over. "Are you the bone-head team?" the boy asked.

"We don't call ourselves boneheads anymore," said Bobby.

"Whatever. Look, I'm supposed to give you a message from my brother, Roland. He's got hives all over his body. He didn't want to mess the team up with his bad breath during the huddles, so he went on the Internet, and this site said he should eat garlic and drink vinegar, and he got sick something awful and it turns out he's allergic to garlic. He's covered in red bumps."

I would have totally traded all those times I made fun of Roland's breath just to have him there. Eugenia didn't look so great, either. There was no telling if she could survive the full competition, and if she got sick and had to quit, without any alternates we would be disqualified.

Mr. Ripple tapped on his microphone. "Testing," he said. "One-two-three testing."

"Looks like we're it," said Adam. Bobby and I reluctantly took our seats.

The scoreboard blinked to life and flashed the names of the three teams. We had voted to call ourselves the Frogs. It seemed like a good idea at the time, but now that I saw the names the other teams had chosen—Wolves for the academic team and Lions for the honors team—I wasn't so sure.

Adam put his hand out. "Here goes," he said. I placed my hand on top, and Bobby, Salvador, Keisha, and Eugenia piled theirs on.

"On the count of three," said Adam. "One, two, three . . ."

"Go, Frogs!" we yelled.

The Wolves at the academic team table huddled, and then jumped all at once. "Eat frogs!" they yelled.

Eugenia blew her nose. "*Do* wolves eat frogs?"

"If they're desperate," said Salvador.

"What about lions?" she asked.

"Big cats don't waste time on amphibians," he replied.

The Lions at the honors/gifted and talented team table let out a frog-curdling roar, and the kids who came to watch us get eaten alive beat their feet so hard against the bleachers the floor seemed to shake.

"But lions do prey on wolves," said Keisha, raising her voice to be heard above the crowd. "So if wolves eat frogs and lions eat wolves, then technically, lions eat frogs."

"Knock it off," said Adam.

186

The Lions roared again.

It reminded me of the Muppet movie I had seen where Kermit the Frog was dressed like a gladiator. On one side of a fence was the frog; on the other were the lions. This is how Kermit must have felt right before the fence was raised and the big cats pounced.

21 Aphrodite Finds Some Luck

Before you leave for an airport, always make sure to check that you are not still wearing your bunny slippers. This may seem obvious, but trust me, it's the kind of mistake you don't want to make twice.

I glanced down at my pink slippers, threw my bag in the trunk of the taxi, and hopped in. I could always change into the other shoes I'd packed when I got to the airport. "To Boston International," I instructed.

The driver had a double chin and a thick Beantown accent. He checked me out with a squinted eye. "Where are your parents?" he asked. "I don't give rides to runaways."

I showed him a wad of cash. "Take the short route. There'll be a fifty-dollar tip if we make it by two o'clock."

The driver flipped on his meter and pulled into traffic. He made his tip, and I raced to the ticket counter.

"Pittsburgh International Airport . . . next plane," I gasped.

The woman punched keys and scrolled down a computer screen. "Sorry," she said. "There's nothing until nine p.m."

"No," I said. "That will be too late."

The woman scrolled again. "There is a flight at two forty-four, but the gate is on the other side of the terminal. I don't think you'll make it."

"I'll make it," I said, tossing hundred-dollar bills on the counter. "Just give me the ticket."

By the time I got through security and found the gate, they were closing the door.

"Wait!" I shouted.

It was supposed to be a two-hour flight, but we got stuck behind air traffic and didn't land until 5:15 p.m. As the taxi pulled in front of my home, I sensed something was wrong. Mother's truck was gone, but the lights were on inside.

"Wait here," I instructed the cab driver, handing him an extra twenty. "I may need you."

The front door was locked. I peered through the

glass and saw Summer talking on the hallway phone. I rang the bell, and she let me in.

"Hey, Professor Wigglesmith. What are you doing here?"

"A better question is, what are you doing here?"

"Babysitting your little brother. I just set him in his playpen. Your parents went to Carnegie Middle School to watch the Great Math Showdown. I wanted to go, but they're paying twice my normal rate. There's this pair of jeans and I'm dying . . ."

As she rambled, the taxi pulled away. "No!" I screamed.

"That's what I said," Summer continued. "Last year's style isn't even worth it on clearance. Hello?"

"Could your parents come over and give me a lift?" I asked.

"They're at the math competition, too." Summer checked her watch. "Everybody's probably there already."

"But I need a ride!"

"Good luck with that," said Summer. A voice came out of the telephone, and Summer put it back to her ear. "Sorry. It's nobody. Just Professor Wigglesmith."

If I was going to make it to the math competition, I needed to be clever or lucky. I had run out of clever ideas. Where could I find luck at this time of night? I thought about the four-leaf clover tattoo on Mr. Finch's head.

"Everybody can do with a bit o' luck," he had said.

Where was Mr. Finch when I needed him? Mr. Finch! That was it. The pool hall wasn't that far from my house. Maybe he could give me a ride. I borrowed the phone from Summer and called the Shoot-M-Up pool hall.

"Sure, we can take you over," Mr. Finch said. "Give us your address."

Ten minutes later, I heard a terrible roar. Four burly men on motorcycles were revving their motors in front of my house. Their bikes were extra-long chopper-style, with shiny metal wheels and black leather seats. Mr. Finch was perched on a massive bike with a frame on the back.

"Come!" he yelled to me. "Hop on."

I strapped on a helmet and climbed behind Mr. Finch.

"Hold on good," he said. "I don't want you falling off."

I threw my arms around his stomach and held tight. As we raced for the middle school, the wind whipped my hair and stung my cheeks. Still, there was something exciting about the ride that made my whole body tingle. I clung tightly to Mr. Finch until we pulled in front of the middle school. The lot was so packed we parked on the grass. Inside, the bleachers were crammed full of spectators.

"Maybe we should stand in the back," I said.

"Allow me," said Snake. He smiled and his gold teeth sparkled. He went over to a group of middle schoolers sitting in the front row. The students got up and fled the gym. Snake waved us over.

"It's the smile," he said as we took the empty seats. "All I ever have to do is ask."

After we got settled, I explained the rules to Mr. Finch. Each team would be given a math problem and sixty seconds to solve it for five points. If one team missed a question, another team could steal their points with the correct answer.

I noticed Mrs. Underwood sitting behind me. "What's the score?" I asked her.

"If you're here to cheer for the remedial team, you'd better get started," she said. She nodded toward Mindy, Adam, Salvador, Keisha, Eugenia, and Bobby, who were hunched together, quibbling furiously. "They're already behind: 10 to 10 to 0."

22 Mindy Figures it Out

That's it," Adam whispered. "The square root of 96,100 is 310."

The Lions were getting close to the end of their time, and if they didn't answer soon, the Wolves could steal. Salvador was doing this weird fidgeting thing with his glasses; Bobby was fishing his fingers beneath his shirt collar, trying to loosen his necktie; and Eugenia was swaying blankly like she was focusing all her energy on not throwing up. "Are you okay?" I asked her.

Eugenia nodded weakly.

Buzzzzzzzzzz!

"Time's up," said Mr. Ripple. "If the Wolves have the correct answer, they can steal."

"Three thousand, one hundred," answered the captain of the Wolves. His teammates gave him high fives.

"The answer is incorrect," said Mr. Ripple. "Do the Frogs want to wager a guess?"

Adam cleared his throat. After flubbing our first two questions, we were really sweating.

"Three hundred ten?" he said.

"The answer is correct," said Mr. Ripple. "Frogs get the steal for five points."

Loud applause and whistles burst from the bleachers. "Go Frogs!" someone yelled.

Eugenia gasped. "Look!" she cried.

Nothing could have prepared me—there was Dytee, and the gang from the Shoot-M-Up pool hall.

"It can't be," Keisha said.

Dytee smiled and waved. Mr. Finch bent his head down and pointed to his four-leaf clover.

"It's Professor Wigglesmith," Adam said. "And she brought us a good-luck charm."

Dytee had come back, but was it for good or just to watch the math competition? Was she still mad at me for what I said? Now was not the time to think about it. The Wolves looked rattled as they worked on their problem. We needed to concentrate to be ready in case we got a chance to steal. "Don't get distracted," I said, repeating what Miss Brenda would tell me at my baton competitions.

"The answer is seventeen percent," the captain of the Wolves told Mr. Ripple. "We are quite sure of it."

"The answer is correct," said Mr. Ripple. "Five more points puts the Wolves in the lead."

Bobby groaned.

"Shhhh," said Salvador.

"The next question is for the Frogs. When expressing algebraic expressions, what is the correct order of operatives?"

It was one of the things Dytee had taught us to remember by using a memorable phrase, in this case, "Please Excuse My Dad's Awful Skirt." The first letter of each word—PEMDAS—was the sequence necessary to get the answer right.

"The order is parenthesis, exponents, multiplication, division, addition, and subtraction," said Adam.

"The answer is correct," Mr. Ripple said. "After two rounds, the score is as follows: Lions 10; Wolves 15; and Frogs 10."

The audience clapped, whistled, and banged against the bleachers.

"The next question is for the Lions."

Time raced by as we tackled harder and harder math questions. Sometimes my teammates came up with different answers and we had to guess which one of us was right. The Wolves got a question wrong, but nobody could steal. We were trapped in a three-way tie. Then we fell behind by five points.

"The score is: Lions 25; Wolves 25; and Frogs 20," Mr. Ripple announced.

"We're gonna lose," said Bobby.

"After all our work. It's not right," said Keisha.

Eugenia blew her nose.

"Don't give up," said Adam. "We've come this far. We can still win."

"The next question," said Mr. Ripple, "is for the Lions."

Suddenly Eugenia's head disappeared below the table. She had it between her knees.

"I think I'm going to throw up," Eugenia said.

"Don't," I begged. "Hang on. We need you."

"I'm going to be sick," said Eugenia. "I'm not kidding."

"You're just too hot because it's so stuffy in here. Let's get your sweater off," I said, helping her remove it.

"Ready now?" asked Mr. Ripple.

I spread the sweater in Eugenia's lap. "If you get sick, vomit into your lap."

Eugenia vomited into her lap. She regurgitated on command so quickly, I wondered if she had been a cow in a prior life. Why hadn't I thought to tell her *not* to vomit instead? The smell wafted up and assaulted the team.

"Oh, man," cried Salvador. He jumped from his chair.

"Is there a problem?" asked Mr. Ripple.

I made the hand signal for a time-out.

"The Frogs have requested a time-out period," announced Mr. Ripple. "According to the rules, each team is entitled to take only one five-minute time-out during the match, provided no question is pending. This will be the Frogs' only time-out." He placed the microphone in its holder and left to talk to the scorekeeper.

"Now what do I do?" Eugenia asked me. Her face was still held over her lap. The pool of vomit was being absorbed into her sweater. I used a dry sleeve of the sweater to wipe her mouth.

"Roll up your sweater, throw it in the bathroom trash, and wash your face," I said, helping her up. "If you're not back in five minutes, we forfeit. So hurry."

"I'll try," said Eugenia. She stumbled away, clutching her bunched-up sweater.

As the seconds passed, my heart was beating so hard I wondered if people could see my chest pounding.

Mr. Ripple came over. "One minute," he warned. He looked at his watch as the time counted down with no sign of Eugenia.

So this was how it would end: defeat by forfeit.

Dytee got up from her seat and started walking toward Mr. Ripple, who was paying too much attention to his watch to even notice. "Excuse me," she said when she was standing right beside him. Mr. Ripple's eyes bugged out like he had seen a ghost. "You! I thought you'd left."

"May I inquire as to the nature of the problem?"

I was never so glad to see anyone. "Eugenia's sick," I told her. "She puked and had to go wash her face. I don't think she's going to make it back in time."

"Who are your alternates?" Dytee asked.

"Bobby, Mindy, and Hunter were the alternates," said Adam, "but Mindy and Bobby are already filling in for Roland and LeeAnn, and Hunter didn't show."

"No alternates?" said Mr. Ripple. "That's too bad. You'll have to forfeit."

Dytee took a step back, and as bad as I felt for the team, I felt even worse for her. After all the effort she had put into us, her math wizzes were about to be math fizzes.

"I'd like to see the list of alternates," Dytee said.

Adam stood. "But, I—"

"The list, please," she said to Mr. Ripple. "The Frogs are entitled to call any alternate listed."

"You want the list, fine," said Mr. Ripple. "Call all of the missing teammates. Then the crowd can stare as nobody steps forward and you can further embarrass the poor students who did show. Maybe then you will be satisfied." Mr. Ripple stormed over to the scorekeeper's table to get the list.

"He's right," I said. "There's no point."

"Trust me," said Dytee.

Mr. Ripple rushed back and handed her a clipboard with the list of names on it.

"Now a pen," Dytee demanded. He handed her his ballpoint, and she put a line through Hunter's name. Then she added her own name to the list.

Mr. Ripple took the paper and chuckled. "Nice try, but I don't think so."

"What's going on?" Bobby asked.

"Professor Wigglesmith just joined the team," I told him.

The edge of Mr. Ripple's lip began to quiver. "This is not funny."

"I'm serious," said Dytee.

"Obviously," Mr. Ripple told her, "teachers are not allowed to participate in the math competition."

"But," I said, "she doesn't teach here anymore."

Mr. Ripple looked so totally ticked he could have been a time bomb. "You have to be an eighth grader to participate."

"No," said Dytee. "I read the rules, and they state that you must be no older than thirteen years of age and reside in the area serving the Carnegie School District. I am, and I do, so unless Eugenia returns, I will be the sixth Frog."

Mr. Ripple stomped his foot. "That's not fair," he objected.

"Not fair?" said Dytee. "One might say it's unfair that you write the questions since you know your students' strengths and weaknesses. I don't like to fuss. I'm doing this to give the Frogs a chance to finish the competition. I will fill the sixth seat, but I have no intention of giving them the answers."

"Fine," said Mr. Ripple. "There are only three questions left." He returned to the microphone. "For the Frogs, Professor Aphrodite Wigglesmith will be replacing Eugenia Billsworth Smith."

A wave of murmurs rolled across the audience. The Lions and the Wolves stared at Dytee with widened eyes and dropped mouths.

Mr. Ripple raised his hand to quiet the crowd. "I will now give the Lions their final question."

The Lions huddled and worked. Occasionally, one would look over, and Dytee would wink or give a thumbs-up. The looks on their faces were priceless. When their sixty seconds were almost up, an argument broke out, and the Lions' captain pinned a team member against the table.

Mr. Ripple rushed to restore order. In the midst of it, the buzzer rang. Mr. Ripple's hair was still messed up when he returned to the microphone. He took out a handkerchief and dabbed at his forehead. "Do the Wolves have the answer for the steal?" he asked.

"We do not," said the Wolves' captain.

My team was half listening and half concentrating on finding the right answer.

"I think that's it," I whispered to Adam.

"There's no time to check," said Salvador.

"We've got nothing to lose by guessing," said Adam.

"Frogs," said Mr. Ripple, "we're waiting. Do you have the answer?"

"The answer is negative 4.7?" said Adam, more like a question than an answer.

"I'm sorry, that answer is"— Mr. Ripple glanced at the answer card and his voice rose an octave— "correct."

The auditorium shook again with clapping and stomping.

The bikers yelled above the roar. "Lions and Wolves go sing the blues, because you know you're gonna lose!" They sprang from their seats like cheerleaders and made victory signs. "Go, Frogs!"

"That will be enough!" Mr. Ripple shouted. Feedback screeched through the air and silenced the crowd. "The score is tied at 25 all. This is the last question for the Wolves. What is the formula for calculating the perimeter of a rectangle?"

An overconfident Wolf blurted out the answer for calculating the perimeter of a triangle by mistake: Perimeter = side A, plus side B, plus side C.

"The answer is incorrect," said Mr. Ripple. "Do the Frogs have an answer?"

The Wolves had responded so quickly that we were still huddled.

"If we pick up this steal," Bobby whispered, "I think we can win. Can you believe it?"

"This is gonna be so sweet," Keisha said. "I can smell the victory."

"Not so fast," I said. "Does anyone know the answer?"

"It's two times side A plus side B," said Adam.

"No, that's not right," said Salvador, adjusting his glasses.

"I'm the captain and I say it is," said Adam.

I folded my arms and sat back. "My vote is with Adam."

"Why should we care who your vote is with?" Salvador asked me. "You haven't solved a single problem."

"Your answer?" Mr. Ripple demanded.

"And just because Adam is the captain," said Salvador, "it doesn't mean he's right."

"Leave him alone," said Bobby. "Everyone but you agrees."

"That doesn't make his answer right."

Buzzzzzzzzzz!

"Time is up," said Mr. Ripple.

It was too late to answer. The boos hit us like tomatoes.

"Quiet down," Mr. Ripple snapped. "If the Lions know the answer, they can steal."

"That's it," said Bobby. "We're doomed. If they pick up the steal, it's over."

The captain of the Lions smiled. "The answer is two times side A plus side B."

"Correct!" cried Mr. Ripple.

The crowd erupted, and Mr. Ripple did not move to quiet it.

"We're losers," said Bobby.

"Not complete losers," said Adam. "We have one question left, and if we get it right, we'll pull into second place. That's better than third."

I looked at Dytee to see how she was handling the defeat. The experiment was definitely over and the results were in: we would never be math wizzes. But Dytee was on her way to Mr. Ripple. He covered the microphone as she whispered in his ear. His smile dropped like a dodgeball falling from an airplane. When Dytee returned, she was the one smiling.

"There has been a challenge. I stand corrected. Because the answer failed to indicate that side A plus side B must be enclosed in parentheses, it is not correct. The Lions do not get the steal, and the score remains tied."

A large woman in the third row fainted onto a row of fifth graders, and the television crew rushed over to get it on film.

"The last question of the night is for the Frogs," said Mr. Ripple.

Timothy suddenly jumped up from his seat at the top of the bleachers.

"Wait!" he yelled. He crisscrossed to the floor and darted over to where Dytee had been sitting. He put his hand on Mr. Finch's head and rubbed his four-leaf clover tattoo. Then he scampered back to his seat. "Okay! Go ahead."

The crowd burst into laughter. While they were laughing, Mr. Ripple shuffled his index cards and chose the last question.

"This is a word problem," he said, reading the card. "Listen carefully. Thirty-five students attend a dance. Nobody may dance with anyone shorter than him- or herself. Sixty percent of the students are over six feet tall. How many couples can dance?"

Our team jotted down the problem.

"Sixty seconds," Mr. Ripple reminded us.

The Frogs huddled.

"If sixty percent of the students are over six feet tall," Adam whispered, "that means forty percent are shorter."

"So only that forty percent could find partners not taller than them," said Keisha.

"There are 35 couples," Bobby added. "Forty percent of 35 is 14. So the answer must be 14 couples."

"I don't know," said Salvador. "What do you think, Professor Wigglesmith?"

"No," I said. "Don't tell us."

"Mindy's right," Dytee said. "I leveled the playing field for you, but you have to win—or lose—on your own."

"I agree," said Adam.

"Wish us good luck?" I asked Dytee.

"You don't need to rely on luck," she told me. "You've got a knack for word problems. Visualize the problem. I know you can solve it."

I closed my eyes and concentrated. *Nobody may dance with anyone shorter than him- or herself.* I imagined dancing with Adam under the sparkling disco ball. I was taller than most of the kids at school, but so was Adam. I had never considered which one of us was taller than the other before. Of course, no two people are exactly the same height, no matter how tiny the difference. *Nobody may dance with anyone shorter than him- or herself.*

"Time's up," said Mr. Ripple.

Adam breathed deeply. I watched as his gaze went to his parents at the top row of the bleachers. He stood. "The answer is—"

"Wait!" I jumped up and cupped a hand over Adam's ear, "It's a trick question," I whispered. "With every couple, one of them is going to be shorter than the other. If nobody can dance with anyone shorter than him- or her-self, then nobody can dance at all."

He smiled. "Go ahead. You tell them."

I opened my mouth, but no sound came out. What if I was wrong? What if the audience burst out in laughter and the kids at school called me an idiot for the rest of my days? Then I remembered something Dytee told me: *Making a mistake doesn't mean you're stupid; it just means you're human.* She was right. The people who were important to me, my real friends, like Dytee and Adam, knew I wasn't a bonehead. More important, I knew it, too. So what if I got it wrong? So what if people laughed? I still had "infinite potential." I *was* the kind of girl who could land on her feet. "The answer," I said, "is zero."

Mr. Ripple's jaw dropped, and he stuttered out the result: "Correct."

First place! We jumped and hopped around like we really were frogs. I latched onto Adam, and we got pressed into a huge group hug. Spectators from the bleachers ran onto the floor, whooping and hollering.

People in the crowd supporting the Lions or the Wolves began to chant, "Rematch. Rematch. Rematch."

I looked for Dytee, but the crowd was rushing against me. Suddenly a burly biker pulled me off my feet and tossed me onto his shoulders like I was a rag doll. All the Frogs were on shoulders. Spectators had brought cans of Silly String and were spraying them. A television camera was getting it in the lens. There was so much confusion, so many people; I couldn't find Dytee anywhere. She was gone.

23 Aphrodite Figures It Out

They say that if everybody is special then nobody is, but I think that's a load of doggie doo-doo. Can't everyone be special in their own different way? Some people are math geniuses and some people are baton geniuses. Other people are really good at throwing up neatly into their laps, like Eugenia, or at caring enough about their friends to eat garlic and drink vinegar for them to try to get rid of their bad breath, like Roland. Isn't it all genius? That's what I figured out at the Great Math Showdown.

The next day, I went to say good-bye. Even though school wasn't quite over, it was the last day the remedial math class would be meeting; Principal DeGuy had been so impressed by the Frogs' first place win that he said everyone in the class had already earned an A. The students decided to throw a party to celebrate. They had used the two-hundred-dollar prize from Right Type Office Supply Store to buy drinks, snacks, and a pizza pie for each student. Timothy arranged his pepperoni to make the number 3.14 so he could call his a pizza pi.

I helped myself to a slice of veggie lovers and got out my folder. "I have something for you," I said. I handed each member of the class a certificate on which I had inscribed my favorite math saying: *Not everything that can be counted counts, and not everything that counts can be counted.*—Albert Einstein.

Some of the students who hadn't gotten a chance yet to put on their "Why Math Matters to Me" presentations decided to do them. Bobby showed the class how to use math to calculate strikes and spares in bowling, and how to knock down a row of math books using his new bowling ball. LeeAnn—who really had been missing practice to wash her cat, which it turned out had some weird skin problem that they had to rush it to the vet for on the night of the Great Math Showdown—explained how she could beat a role-playing video game ten percent faster by calculating probabilities during a quest.

Holding a gleaming baton trophy in one hand, Mindy read from an index card about how baton twirlers apply torque to make the baton turn in a circular motion. She explained that force, speed, and angular velocity are essential to twirlers. Then she used her baton to show off some basic spins.

"Excellent," I said. "When math concepts are used to help explain a physical phenomenon, such as how a baton works, we call it physics." I stepped on the stool so I could write the term high on the board, but it didn't make a sound. Mindy turned to Roland, and he gave her a mysterious thumbs-up.

Timothy was the last student to present. "Math matters to me because there are a lot of really funny math jokes. Ten cats were in a boat and one jumped out. How many were left? None! The rest were copy cats. Get it?"

"Knock, knock," said Roland.

"Who's there?" Timothy answered.

"Police."

"Police who?"

"Police stop telling lame jokes."

Finally, Adam went to the back of the room and pulled a bag from the closet. *Shhhhh* could be heard around the room. He handed the bag to Mindy, who handed it to me.

"Last night," Adam explained, "after we won the

math competition, we wanted to thank you. We'll be going to Carnegie High School in the fall. You'll be going back to Harvard."

"We wanted to give you something to remember us," said Mindy.

"Just give it to her," said Roland.

"Anyway," Mindy continued, "here it is."

I blushed and said, "Thank you." The package was about six inches square and wrapped in silver with a pink bow. Inside was a plastic frog. It had a wide mouth and a long red tongue that flew out when I squeezed. The class had glued feathery wings to it.

"Because you taught us that frogs can fly," said Adam.

My smile was so wide there was barely room on my face for it. Then the bell rang, and the students raced from their seats like they were on fire. Most screamed their good-byes on their way out. A small group risked being late for their next class to give me a personal send-off.

Mindy was the last to go. She hesitated, as if gathering her thoughts. "I guess this is it."

"My plane doesn't leave until tomorrow."

"All the same, I'm going to say this now, to make sure it gets said. I apologize for being mean and telling you to go back to Harvard. I didn't really want you to go. I was angry because Adam danced with you instead of me. I wanted to hurt you, but I ended up hurting everybody, because you really did leave."

"It wasn't just you," I admitted. "I would have had to leave anyway. Harvard wanted me back. How could I say no?"

"So you're happy at Harvard?"

The question took me off guard. "I'm . . ." *What was the way to describe it?* "I'm fulfilling my destiny."

Mindy looked down at her shoes. "Remember when I said that we couldn't be friends, that it would be too weird? It wasn't true. You were the best friend I ever had." Then she hugged me. It was not a more-arms-than-chest hug like I sometimes saw Mindy give Jordeen, Veronica, or Summer, but a long I'm-going-to-miss-my-best-friend hug that required me to stop breathing for a second so I wouldn't ruin it.

"It was my sister," said Father as he hung up the phone that evening. "She's down with the flu again and wanted to know if I could go over and help her with the little ones."

"Go ahead," said Mother. "You can bring along the casserole that's in the freezer."

I had just finished packing my bag and bringing it

downstairs to set near the door so I would be ready to leave first thing in the morning.

"I'll be back as soon as I can," said Father, grabbing his car keys.

He wasn't gone five minutes when the phone rang. It was a customer with a plumbing emergency.

"Sorry," said Mother. "Would you keep an eye on Hermy for me?"

I pulled a chair next to his playpen. Hermy was sound asleep, sucking his pacifier in and out as he breathed. I stroked his hair. Ten minutes passed. Twenty minutes. An hour. I wished he would wake up so I wouldn't be alone. That way, I wouldn't have to think about what I was doing—returning to Harvard.

I turned on a television show about predatory insects, but my mind kept wandering back to Harvard. *Was I happy there?* That's what Mindy had asked. I could do important work there. I could utilize my talents there, like my professors wanted me to. But was I happy? It was such a simple question; I could hardly believe I had never considered it before.

I thought about it for another hour, until Mother finally came home. "Someone flushed a sock," she reported. "When will they learn that even a toilet needs a little respect to function?" She headed upstairs to shower, like she always did after a plumbing job.

I waited until she was dressed. We sat in the den, across from her collection of Golden Plunger Awards for Plumbing Excellence. I got straight to the point. "Would you be too disappointed if I decided I didn't want to be a famous mathematician anymore?"

The color drained from her face. "But it's all you've ever wanted," she said. "Principal DeGuy, the people at the gifted testing office, your teachers and professors, they've all told us it is what's best for you, your destiny."

"But destiny, if there is such a thing, is what brought me to Carnegie Middle School. Destiny isn't just something that happens to you. Like Father says, 'Life is what you make it.'"

She took my hand and held it on her lap. "It is," she agreed, nodding as she spoke. "Of course it is."

For a few moments we were both silent as we appreciated the magnitude of what had just taken place. Finally, I asked, "You're not too disappointed?"

"A bit surprised, yes; disappointed, no. But if you don't go back to Harvard, what will you do?"

I had absolutely no idea. Suddenly my future was a wide-open field and, regardless of my IQ, I could spin

215

through that field as fast or as slow as I wanted. I didn't have to be anything except me.

It's funny how the smallest things can make the biggest difference in a person's life. Fate and destiny were qualities that were hard to calculate. Like the sock that Mother had to unclog the night before I was supposed to go back to Harvard. If that sock hadn't ended up in someone's pipes, Mother might not have left me alone with the time that I needed to think. Of all the possibilities in the universe, it was, for the third—*and final*—time, a toilet that changed my life, forever.

That night, before I went to sleep, I counted all of the cash I had accumulated. Then I cleared a spot in the center of my bedroom, hugged Hershey Bear to my chest, and spun. Around and around and around. And when I stopped, at that exact moment when my brain hadn't yet caught up to my body and it felt like I was still spinning, I stumbled upon what I wanted to do.

"Three more steps," I told Mindy. It had taken an entire week to get my surprise ready for her. Halfway through the drive there, I had made her put on a blindfold. Now we were standing on the sidewalk, getting ready for the big reveal.

"Now?" asked Mindy.

"Now," I said.

She pulled the scarf off her eyes and was so startled she almost stumbled.

The Baton Barn had never looked better. It had been repainted flamingo pink. Batons poked from the ground lining the path to its doors. Across the face of it was a huge sign: UNDER NEW MANAGEMENT.

"I made Miss Brenda a better offer," I said. "So you can keep taking lessons as long as you want."

The crowd behind us began to whoop and cheer. Our families, the math team, the teachers from Carnegie Middle School, the guys from the Shoot-M-Up pool hall, Miss Brenda's students, even the news reporters—everyone we knew had turned out for the surprise.

"What a great story of friendship," said the reporter from the *Carnegie Signal Item*. "You two are amazing. You should write a book together: *From Bonehead to Infinity,* or *Aphrodite Wigglesmith and the Toilet's Flush.*"

"Only a total genius would read that hilarious book," said Timothy.

The whole thing was captured for the evening news: Mindy jumping up and down, screaming for joy; the other baton students doing cartwheels; Mr. Finch bending over so people could rub his lucky tattoo; Timothy telling me another one of his amusing jokes;

217

me telling him my Einstein joke; Timothy laughing; me calling dibs on him.

"What's dibs?" he asked.

"It's a girl thing," Mindy told him.

I had never noticed how cute he was. Maybe I could convince him to sign up for baton lessons. Now that I owned the Baton Barn, I would have to figure out how to twirl. I already had experience as a math teacher, but being a baton teacher was going to be a whole new challenge. Sure, I was still a math genius, but that wasn't *all* I was anymore.

The batons lining the walkway had sparkly streamers on their ends. I pulled one out and drew the symbol for infinity in the air with it. Then I placed my hand around the center of the shaft. A formula came to me. I calculated the height of the Baton Barn, the distance to the other buildings, and the wind speed. Then I spread my legs out for balance, lowered the baton, and flung it in the air.

It flew like it had wings—up, up, up, three stories high. While I watched the baton tumble to earth, Mindy grabbed my arm and pulled me over a few feet. She extended my hand, palm up. The baton landed perfectly, filling the void in my palm between my life line and heart line.

218